Rompolicious

Laurice Watson

Order this book online at www.trafford.com
or email orders@trafford.com

Most Trafford titles are also available at major online book retailers.

Note for Librarians: A cataloguing record for this book is available from Library
and Archives Canada at www.collectionscanada.ca/amicus/index-e.html

Printed in Victoria, BC, Canada.

ISBN: 978-1-4269-0379-3

*Our mission is to efficiently provide the world's finest, most comprehensive book publishing
service, enabling every author to experience success. To find out how to publish your
book, your way, and have it available worldwide, visit us online at www.trafford.com*

Trafford rev. 08/24/09

North America & international
toll-free: 1 888 232 4444 (USA & Canada)
phone: 250 383 6864 ♦ fax: 812 355 4082

This book is dedicated to all the men and women I've loved,

And for bMg,

Thank you for Rompolicious.

Acknowledgments

This book has been written over a long period of time, many individuals are a part of its end result, you were an inspiration and a support found from the smallest to grandest of moments. My love and great thanks to each of you.

Special thanks to Alex for your unfailing support and getting me moving again, Stacy and Birgit for editing, Liz and Holly for the photography, Steven for the cover art and to all of you who read a chapter, your feedback and encouragement in the face of my doubts. To my fiancé, who has been there from the books conception through to every decision, step and choice that arose. To my family, I thank you for always seeing me bigger then I had let myself be, I did it!

As to the style, well this too has evolved over time and after exposure to some fun and influencing authors whose writings each gave me something to consider.

Eve Ensler; her lack of fear, her courage and directness in addressing the un-addressable got me through some moments I wanted to change or be meek with words.

Chelsea Handler; after a hilarious visit into her experiences, I decided to write what I knew using both my imagination and my own experiences.

It all came together as it was meant to - xo

Contents

The Why of the Book

Assuming you have at least one great friend you can talk about anything with, you will know what it's like when they are sexually frustrated. If the two of you are in the same boat, watch out. Why is it that sexually frustrated people talk about it? One would think you would want to avoid the topic when you are not getting any, instead of being reminded that you are not. Even going further and talking of all the other great sexual things you have done in the past that you are not doing now. It's torture and I don't know why it happens but it does.

I was in this situation, when I began to write this book. I had befriended a woman of extreme natures. She was more sexually active than I was, and more casual about it. That said, we still managed to entertain each other. She had a great body and loved to dance around showing off her latest dance class moves. Being that it was Latin dance classes she was taking, I always wanted to go out and just fuck someone silly after watching her try out some of those moves that looked like they were made for the bedroom.

This inevitably began a conversation about sex, or about our lack of it. We would begin resurrecting our most recent escapades so we could live vicariously through each other until one of us experienced our next encounter.

I would have to say that as fun as it was, neither one of us was a good influence in supporting the other into having the meaningful relationships we actually desired. Being around sexually oriented people just offers permission to be more outrageous than your last adventure. This was not competitive- I would say it was more inspiration.

In deciding to take up writing once again I had hopes that writing about sex would fill the void that lack of sex had left behind. I figured I would get some variety in getting off and my vibrator would not become my best friend.

It started off working out great. I had asked a number of people to share their stories and was met with a great response. Some casual and some people were more than willing to share things about themselves that I didn't necessarily want to know. Once I got past the awkward, shy, and joking around, I had some really great in-depth conversations about what people liked and had done.

I would have to say, the process was enlightening and I have learned a few things about myself and my body as a woman.

I did not begin writing this book to please anyone else. It may sound selfish, but this book was for me. It had been about accomplishing what I started out to do and it ended up being my sex life for months. I like sex. I like the little Harlequin style books; in most cases – not all- the story was merely a way to the sex scenes. I have begun writing about five books over the past ten years all in that style. This time I found I was writing the sex scenes and then trying to fill in the story around them. After this epiphany, I began to focus on that alone. From there it was an easy step to writing a collection of short stories relating to sex. I started with some of my own experiences and filled in with created stories from previous book attempts combined and rounded out with tidbits of researched stories.

I wrote this book over the course of two years, some chapters and even sections of chapters were written months apart. It was this great collage of moments that for the most part, I really didn't have a lot of emotional attachment to anymore. Only when I put it all together and read it in succession did these stories become real again, embarrassingly so in some cases, guilty in others, humorously for many. Considering I could almost be a virgin again it was weird to feel like I had just shagged many men in the span of a couple days.

Each chapter begins with an introduction from me, about my experience or my opinion, and then is followed by a story on the topic. The stories may have been altered due to the memories being fuzzy, having been under the influence or having been present in that moment versus cataloguing for future writing. And yes, the names are in some cases, changed to protect the privacy of those involved.

I found after many interviews that as original as we think we are, many of us have a similar story to tell.

Either way I hope you enjoy it. The best compliment on my writings of this book was my girlfriend telling me she masturbated to it!

1

The Beginning, the Middle and the Others

The men who didn't get their own chapter

$\mathcal{L}$ast night, as I was rounding off the last of the chapters and organizing them, I made a list of all my lovers and wanted to see if anyone didn't make it in the book somehow. Which brought me to this chapter and what I felt was a perfect opener for those whom I did not write into a chapter of their own and giving them honorable mention and first billing so to speak to prove they weren't forgotten.

I realized that some stories just weren't worth the write and in other cases the story just didn't come up before these others that I did write about; maybe there will be a sequel. Don't feel bad for them; it's not necessarily a reflection of my lack of enjoyment of our sex life. They fall into one or more of these three categories;

I only slept with them once

I will start off by telling you I have never had a traditional one night stand. I have never slept with a stranger, and by stranger I mean someone I met that night and never saw again. I have slept with men who I have known for years and yet they are still strange to me. I only slept with them once because for one reason or another, it just never happened again.

The one hit wonder: Cullen – thanks for introducing me to having my toes sucked, he was the only guy I ever went home from a bar with. After swallowing up my ordered drink; a Sloe Gin and Seven, through my straw in less then five seconds, he challenged me: "I betcha couldn't do that again". I proceeded to show him how cool I thought I was, by doing it again for him. Never challenge an Irish girl like that, it's just mean and unnecessary, we will do it every time. It is some kind of innate response.

I remember being on his sofa, I don't know how we moved to the bed but we did. I don't remember the progression, but I clearly remember thinking; Oh my God, don't put my feet - that have been in shoes all night -in your mouth, and yet not being able to complete the thought or stop him because he did just that. I was instantly in awe and willingly to do whatever he wanted.

He was the only guy I ever sent flowers to after sex. That's probably because I was scarred by the experience; I had remembered his house number incorrectly and after telling the flower shop to just leave them at my next guess, I really don't know if he ever got them.

The special occasion lay: James - It was one of those stereotypical settings a soap opera could not set up better; cold winter night, cabin, booze and two healthy, single people in the same bed having just toasted in a new year. Enough said!

The 'Please stay; I'll break my vow of celibacy': Stuart – pathetic! I had made a vow to be celibate for a year; nine months in I started dating a guy who told me he was seriously considering moving to a different province. At eighteen I sincerely thought if I gave up my vow, he'd stay for me. He didn't.

The guilt lay and last example of one timers: Greg- my high school graduation. It's hard to feel all that amorous after being humiliated in front of your entire graduating class as my friend Brent shouted out a charming little rhyme that was interlaced with my name and 'everyone gets a piece' – which for the record, was not true. He was a rhyming kind of guy however and that's what he came up with for me. I had gone to my Graduation with my boyfriend of one month. When I got back from my walk of shame across the room having retrieved my lottery ticket prize; I couldn't even look him in the eye. We had sex that night, he'd got us a suite, and I, like many stupid teenagers felt like I owed him for both the embarrassment and the money output. Needless to say, we broke up very soon after and he went back to his ex, and I went back to having secret affairs.

Secret Rendezvous

Sleeping with a guy once or periodically for months and not being able to talk about it with my friends was not uncommon for me. The most exciting part was often the drama of keeping it hidden, once that was all gone, there generally wasn't much more to it. I really only had two official boyfriends between sixteen (the age I lost my virginity) and twenty. In case you are doing the math, yes one of them was Greg, the one month guy above. Mix alcohol and a sexual heredity together with no boyfriend, you get a promiscuous young woman who liked her affairs to be discrete. I will acknowledge that guys found it easy to be around me; this made girls jealous and gave them supposed reason to be protective of their men around me. It was generally insecurity versus justified. I didn't sleep with my friends boyfriends, not while they were dating anyways.

To give credit where it's due amongst my affairs, in high school there was Todd, who took the time and patience, sweetheart that he was, to show me how to give a great hand job, and who I also learned all about the joys of rug burn with. I enjoyed him; there was a lot of laughter, spontaneity and secret smiles in class during our brief, secret and forbidden affair. I had a friend who liked him but she wasn't willing to give it up, I was, I did. It didn't last long. She never found out.

Matt I also kept secret because we went to school together and I hated gossip. He discovered my erogenous shoulder zone and left me obviously bruised by his generous attention. It gave an entirely new meaning to hicky.

The hockey player that I should probably be more embarrassed over the booty call action that played out over a year. I won't go into more story then that.

There was Jay, the one who was secret because he was the Ex of my girlfriend Mac – again my bad! She found out, was pissed with good reason but got over it when she slept with Wayne, a guy I liked. Teenagers are so cruel and yet the justice of it all taught me a lesson

Ah Wayne, the artist who I will always have a soft spot for. When he ended it, he married the next girl he was with. Here is as good a place as any to tell you that this is not uncommon with me, I am not positive on this number but I think its possible that 42.8% of the men I have slept with, within a year, married or got pregnant the woman they dated after me.

Into everyone's life – mine in this case, people are there for a reason, season or a lifetime. These secret guys were a season, the one nighters; a reason, and the story makers in the chapters to follow; a lifetime.

Before we go there though lets round out this chapter reflecting on one last category.

The Rebounders

This is the sad group, not because they are not great men, just in where they fell into my life. I never gave them my whole self. I was their girlfriend but in each case I was not yet over someone else and they were cheated of good story making.

The first was after a devastating breakup, I cannot believe I am saying this but I had to argue my way into sleeping with him. Then sex was the only thing that kept me sane and the only place I allowed any feeling into my life. I learned a lot being with him, I have no idea what punishment he felt he deserved to have put up with me.

Next was Derek, a guy at work I flirted with. He was a self acknowledged commitment phobic. He only liked to date married women to avoid commitment. Beyond still having feelings for my ex, we were just too different for it to have lasted. I think it is possible he may still hate me.

Last, a man I even talked marriage with when people cannot even picture us having dated when they find out. We lasted through six months of fighting, in that time we took three separate vacations. I think we were just two people madly searching for something different than what we had had before. I went for another round with the ex, he found the wife he was searching for.

After many years I finally acknowledged that **I** am the common denominator in the drama of my life thus far. I have studied psychology; I wanted to be a therapist when I was younger. I have created drama to have a problem to always work on. Being aware of it now, I strive for a different result. This book however is about my past and all the traumas and drama that came from my relations including the men above and the men you will meet over and over again in the chapters to follow. If nothing else, it has been entertaining.

2

Sugarpuss

The first time my eyes faced backward

For the first few years of my sexual experience, I was not secure with my body. I drank a lot to forget about the insecurities that always came up for me, I felt my boobs weren't big enough, I wondered if I had shaved my legs/ bikini line, or what was he thinking right at that moment. God, how dreadful that so many young girls become inflicted with those thoughts because we either had sex earlier then we were ready for or we were competing with a skewed vision of what the perfect woman is supposed to look like based on the medias airbrushed and technically enhanced portrayals that few women, if any, can live up to let alone a teenager.

A great lover can help with this. So can finding something you really enjoy. In this moment I can honestly say I don't remember the first time I received oral gratification, though I definitely remember the first time I couldn't speak during it. I remember the room I was in, I even remember the sheets on the bed.

My girlfriend Loryn, came up with the word sugarpuss a couple years ago, she said tell everyone this new word, lets get it out there. I agree it is a much better word to describe oral, it improves the visual don't you think? It's kinda sassy like she is. Much better than eat me, and shorter than cunnilingus. It defines it for the enjoyment it is, rather than some kind of exam at the dentist chair. So from here on out...

It's not to say I had not enjoyed sugarpuss prior to the moment I so clearly remember with this next man, or to say I had never cum previously during. I do know that from Connor- I learned what I like and with each lover since, what I have wanted them to do.

When I began to write this book I did a few interviews. I wanted to get some perspectives on things I found hard to articulate. In this case; sugarpuss, I enjoyed it more then I could necessarily describe it afterwards. I needed a person who had more experience then me. Since I can't do it to myself... (Sorry, had to pause on that visual) and offering the ladies sugarpuss is something my friend John loves to do, I figured he was a good guy to ask. I called him up and asked him if I could come over and have a wee chat about performing oral from a mans perspective. I wanted to know what he liked to do and what had worked for him.

I think we talked about it for over an hour, we got technical and graphic, drew pictures and used our hands to describe things, surprisingly we both remained on task and nonsexual.

I don't know if you have ever been blessed with someone showing you what a woman's vagina looks like and what some woman's vaginas don't look like. Well I have, even before that interview. In college I went to a party that sold sex toys and paraphernalia, the hostess pulls out a laminated copy of two vaginas and says this is a picture of lucky women, and this is the rest of us. Needless to say, not many women have the pleasure of their clit being anywhere near the opening of their vagina so we must find other ways to be stimulated. I found mine.

When I was fourteen (this part has nothing to do with sex) I went to Florida with my parents and my brother. I remember a few things from this trip, one being the second degree burns I got when I fell asleep by the pool after a dip in the ocean, another our visit to Disneyland where every picture of me shows the perfect stereotype of a bored teenager on a trip with her parents, smart assed, uninterested, arms crossed I don't want to have my photo taken look on my face – truly priceless in retrospect.

The other thing I remember is the day we went shopping at the outlet mall on our way home. I got a couple pairs of pants, some shoes and we got a set of sheets in the clearance bin. They were typical 80's fashion style; they were grey with red, blue and green geometric print. I loved these sheets. Not the print that was on them, I loved the feel of them. I had them for twelve years.

I am in love with my current sheets now as well, but even they don't match up to my memory of those sheets. As ugly as they were, they lasted. They had that great cool quality that's priceless in the summer when it's so hot, they never balled, they held the corners and as time passed and the pattern became dated and embarrassing I could not give them up until I left them behind in a move. Again I have gotten way off topic.

I told you I remembered the sheets, it may seem weird, but perhaps now that you know the history of the sheets it won't seem so odd that I remember the sheets in this particular story.

Back to sugarpuss, we were at home, it was the middle of the day, I had just gotten out of the shower, and we were getting ready to go out somewhere. Time was not an issue so when we began to make out, I could not have cared less that we'd had plans.

There is much from that time that is too distant for me to retrieve the memories, I won't lead you down the explicit tale of how we got from my lips to between my legs, because truthfully I just don't remember, and it doesn't matter. What matters, or the part I wanted to share, was the moment when I ignored judgments, social no-no's and my intense mortification and allowed myself to enjoy (to quote Loryn) meeting my first ass licker.

As he licked my pussy with all his talent and focus, his tongue inched lower and lower, each time I shifted away thinking he just didn't know he was off the mark. Then he got past me before I shifted, I felt the minor panic of having to let him know and then all thoughts were gone, I was speechless, thinking oohh uh, that felt kind of good, but still feeling guilty. I shouldn't let him go there, he must not know, his eyes must be closed, I don't want him to think I'm gross.

Then he began to touch me as well, his finger began to trail over my clit, and then slid down where he traced the entrance of my vagina, his finger followed the path his tongue had previously, tracing down a little too far. He got his finger really wet from both me and his saliva and he began to circle my asshole. All I could think was, why does that feel so good when there is no way anything is going in there.

When I finally gave myself over to his ministrations, my legs straddling his shoulders and spreading as far as they could, my hips lifting to give him any access he wanted, I allowed myself to enjoy the best sugarpuss I had ever had. I got past the judgments, of thinking I was a dirty girl and reveled in the intense tingles shooting all through my body stemming from his attentions, his fingers and his tongue. I embraced the plethora of nerve endings shouting out their glory.

It was the first time I orgasmed from oral alone. My hands itching to join him, as he spread my labia open to feast upon me. He told me how much he loved the taste of me, couldn't get enough, I could feel the dripping juices slide out of me. With his tongue and teeth focusing on vibrating my clit and his fingers rubbing my over sensitized vagina from tip to tat, I was too overwhelmed with sensation to control it, too in the moment to think any longer. I gave myself over to the intensity, clutching at my favorite sheets with my eyes unable to focus as they were rolled back in my eye sockets. I gave over to the best orgasm I had ever had without a penis inside me.

3

Vacation Sex

Sex in a bed that is not your own

Why is it that vacation sex is more often than not some of the greatest sex I've ever had? I won't presume to say the same for everyone, but I highly doubt I am alone in this. Is there more passion because I am not going to see this person again? It's a day, a week a month out of reality so I get to be whoever I want to be knowing I can go home and be the less extroverted personality I normally am?

I honestly don't know the answer however I AM sure that vacation sex HAS been SOME of my best. Though I should clarify that the term vacation is used lightly. I have dated a lot of men in other cities and going to see them, or having them come to see me even though we are still in our own cities, feels like vacation, like a snapshot of time taken out of my regular life. Vacation sex can be equated to a reunion of sorts, a euphoric attitude, happy place, not just a trip to Mexico.

For me it's true that I have had boyfriends where the whole time I have been dating them it was vacation sex. Lucky me, wink wink. Perhaps that is my unconscious reason for dating men that don't live in the same city as me. I love the thrill of reunion, the constant first kisses, the passionate couplings built up from storing.

Back to the traditional meaning though, I feel like I have gotten away with more in vacation sex as well. It's as if normal rules don't apply the same as they would in a regular relationship. I have been more open to further orgy like behavior. I have not swapped partners, though there has been more than one person in my bed having a good time. I have never done that with a boyfriend. I am much less possessive in vacation sex, a free for all.

Good times all around.

I sit here thinking which story I will tell for "vacation sex' So many of my stories can cross over more than one category, as I said, some of the most free sex, the best stories worthy of a chapter were not in my bed at home and I have already written a chapter about them.

We all know that great sex isn't just about the physical but rather about the entire game, the lead up, the naughtiness, the daring- it's all foreplay. I personally am not much for physical foreplay. I love the whole make out party, until I want sex. Then, I want it now not when you're done streaking a wet path from one end of me to the other.

The truth is I am not as promiscuous as it may seem. Many of theses stories are about the same couple of men. And sometimes I wish I had someone else to write about, just for variety. I have only been with four men in the last six years, that's a good portion of my 'fun sex life' time frame. Well it's certainly a huge portion of the sex life I have had where

I wasn't drunk. And I didn't really go on vacations beyond cottages and camping until I was in my late twenty's.

Aha! Got one about me but first a little one that I wasn't part of by choice.

One New Years a big group of my friends all went to Tahoe for a week. There were about twenty-four of us all staying in one great and large house. Surprisingly, many of us had beds. The week was one of great debauchery. I wont go into details of how, but it was extreme. I will go into the details as they pertain to vacation sex.

It was somewhere between the wee hours of two and five a.m. Most people had passed out if they didn't go to bed on their own controlled choice. I was sleeping with my guy when I was awoken by a noise. At first I didn't know what it was. As I became more conscious and tuned into what had awoken me I realized I was listening to a woman moaning, someone in the house was having sex. I lay there listening to the moans that slowly became quite loud. It woke up my guy too and with certainty the whole damn house as we discovered who the culprits were. Without care to who could hear her, Bootygirl was letting us know how much pleasure she was enjoying, 'OHHHHH BIIIILLLLY, oh BILLY…." over and over for what felt like an hour. I am sure that many of the household were all chuckling in bed as we were.

The two of them were obviously having great vacation sex, and not caring if we knew so why not listen. It's not as if we could have put a pillow over our heads and not heard it. So we listened. I won't tell you that it wasn't a turn on, and I wouldn't be surprised if a few others got busy themselves.

Ok, now back to a much more innocent story

It was August of 1994, and the weekend that many were celebrating the twenty-fifth anniversary of Woodstock. Me, I was camping. Not something I really enjoy anymore but I digress as usual.

It was one of the stories that sum up my sex life to date. I am thirty-two years old currently and I have been on very few dates. I say that because I have always dated someone I knew. A friendship that one day became more; it's never felt like 'dates'.

I grew up in a small town, and over the years proceeded to gravitate to other small communities where everyone knows each other. When I look back on my sexual history, I have slept with men that my friends also have on more then one occasion. One ex reminded me of a time when we were dating, and I summarized this point. We were meeting up with friends, we arrived and we walked in and looked around. The part he found amusing and a memory that stuck for him was when I turned to him and said, 'hmm, I think between you and me, we have slept with everyone here."

In the case of the camping trip, there were four of us camping that weekend; two women and two men. Mackenzie and I had been friends since tenth grade. We were 'Da Girls' a play off of the way guys would say "Da Bears' football team. We were easy to be around, we were not real girly girls, and we could drink beer and hang out in our sweats with the guys. We were not afraid of a little dirt and we could both build a fire.

The two guys; Jay and Rob had never met before even though both of them had been in our lives for awhile. They were from different crowds. Mackenzie had previously slept with both of them; one was her ex –Jay and then Rob, at a party one night. I had slept with one – Jay, her ex, which I alluded to in Chapter One. We were well past that at this point, and Rob had been a good friend of mine for years that I had prided myself on being one of the only women he could call friend that he had not slept with.

Until that weekend. Before I get into that though, I need to say that this was one weekend where my memory is such that the girls were the more capable of the group. I have never seen two men have such a time putting up a freakin tent, and I am sure to this day their memory of it would be different. In the end we had brought three tents. We decided that we would sleep in two and use the other; the biggest one, as a food tent.

The first day after all the tents were up we assigned tents – knowing that the two guys would not share a tent, left it up to us to partner up one girl one guy each tent. At this point, no one was actually dating anyone, each other, or otherwise, we were four single friends going camping.

Mac and I sat on the picnic table with a drink in hand and made a little pact. For me, having had a past with her ex that was awkward territory I didn't want repeated, and having an attraction I had been denying for years to Rob, we agreed I was bunking with him.

We also agreed that if one of us kissed either of the guys ('cause even when its not planned, anything is possible after a couple drinks) we would pay the other a quarter; if we had sex it was a loonie. With the pact in place we drank and sang and did what teenagers do when camping.

I will get back to the details but I think its best to keep you as unaware as she was at first, so I am going to go Tarentino on your ass and tell the story backwards.

The next morning we packed up what we wanted for the day and headed first to the showers to freshen up. When we were done and back at the car I reached into my pocket and plunked a coin into her shirtfront pocket.

Her jaw dropped "No way!!"

I laughed and said "Yes way!"

That was about all we could say because the guys had finished up too and were joining us. We drove down the road, I forget where we were going or why we had stopped but when we did, something tells me it had to do with changing a tire but anyways, Mac for whatever reason went into her pocket.

"Holy Shit, this is a Loonie"

Thinking *her* looney I'm sure, Jay asked what the fuck she was talking about

She just stood there staring at me and it was then that I realized before she even said it,

"I thought it was a quarter"

I laughed out loud and had to suppress further outburst so I wouldn't have to explain her expression or my uncontrollable laughter.

When she got me alone finally having managed to distract the guy's curiosity she was like, "WHAT HAPPENED"?

Now remember, I was nineteen so the innocence of this story *is* the story versus the erotica it was not. I mean seriously – we were camping, sleeping on the ground in a tent we couldn't even stand up in.

I answered her, "After I went to bed, you guys stayed up. While I listened to you guys as I was trying to warm up the ice cold sleeping bag I geared up my courage and thought this is my chance to stop being just friends".

When he came in, after he got settled some, I pretty much jumped him, crawled on top of him.

He asked me if I was sure I wanted to do this

I was like "YES'

"But we are friends" – (ok so this is years later, but it was some comment like that and I commend him for it)

From there I got bruises on my knees while I enjoyed my first ride with him. It wasn't spectacular. But with due respect we were in a freakin tent and both of us were drunk.

We had sex only the one time that weekend, part of it was the novelty of it, the pent up frustration on my part and the knowledge Mac was going to flip out. I didn't care, after the release of tension, the rest the weekend was fun.

I read a book this year entitled 'He's Just Not That Into You'. After only the first chapter I had already laughed out loud, a lot. When I read it and thought about this story I think, he just wasn't into me. But the truth is, I just didn't fucking care, I wanted to have sex with him. Coupled with; he's a guy, I only wanted sex, wasn't asking to date, I got what I wanted that night without further questions and the added bonus of the look on Macs' face with the loonie was priceless.

Over the next few years he and I had sex again a few times, we joked it was a once a year thing in-between significant others, a fall back bootie call – but that is another chapter entirely. He too, last time we spoke – is happily married.

This chapter read and edited by a friend inspired her to take up the pact and when I went away for a weekend inflation came in and she said, 'will you owe me five dollars or twenty when you come home…'

4

Balconies

Voyeurism power

*a*re you into voyeurism, or performing for others? I have had sex on a balcony more times than I thought I would ever say. There is most definitely a thrill to it. A desire to put on a little show, perhaps vamp it up more then usual. My first time was when I was in my early twenties. I remember being in a silk and lacy black bra and panty set and it was chilly out. I remember feeling my nipples hard within my bra and aching to be warmed up by the man I was with. I love knowing you are going to have sex and yet letting your lover lead the show.

I am a Scorpio and true to form I do love sex. I know when I want it and I know how to get it. That said, sometimes it's important to let your lover think it's their idea, pretending he is in charge.

That first time, the experience was sexy. It was November and although not yet snowing, it was not weather to be out in your panties. I don't recall how I got from clothed to exposing my undies though I do very much remember when he first put his hands on me, when he kissed me, when our tongues met. The chill carried over to everything lending an interesting contradiction to the heat we were generating.

The second time was at a party, in the wee hours when few were left. We slipped out and enjoyed each others scenery. Not generally a performer for others, I thought fuck it, why not and ignored knowing someone could see us!

Another experience came (no pun intended yet) with John, at the end of our lengthy discussion on oral sex; the logistics and preferences. You had to know when I said previously 'we both remained on task and nonsexual' that it was inevitable there was going to be an after topic sex session. Who could be that strong and not go there, who'd want to? It was hot and though we never had sex on the balcony, the oral was a great prelude.

My name is Shanekwa, I am 26 years old and I am an alcoholic. I don't go to meetings and I don't plan to. As every alcoholic will tell you at some point, it's under control. I am single, no kids and it doesn't ever affect my work, I just can't remember the last day I didn't have a drink. This is my story.

It was a hot summer day in July. An average day in my world for the most part, but it was also a Friday. I had come home from work, I work at a factory, and I am a secretary. After changing into a bikini, I poured my standard half and half, vodka and seven and sauntered out to the balcony. I live in a small neighborhood where you can't go to the corner store without seeing someone you know. It's different from the small town I grew up in, but only in geography.

The balcony is my sanctuary, where I go most days after work to enjoy the sunshine and wait for my roommate to get home. I either suntan or sit in the chair and watch the people walking by on the street hoping they won't notice me and interrupt my peace, my unwind time. I am good at my job, but I don't get a lot of satisfaction from it, it's easy for me and doing something all day that you don't really enjoy, is draining. I enjoy my after work drinks. Most days I go out there, lay out a towel and lie down on my stomach undo the top of my bikini and wait for my roommate to wake me up and join me for a drink.

Keesha is my roommate. We met and moved in together a year ago. Both of us stepping out on our own in a way, becoming independent. This wasn't the first time either of us had lived with someone but somehow this was different, more grown up. We have become great friends, and she is also my enabler. I would never presume to tell anyone she drinks too much, because she matches me drink for drink. We have fun; she makes it alright for me to do it. With her there, I don't have to drink alone or admit I can't go without. Everyone has issues we hide from; the drink makes them go away for awhile.

On this day, lying out on my towel sipping my drink I thought, life is good. It was one of those moments that still happen periodically for me, when I realize I am an adult. In that moment, I looked around at the apartment that we had made into a home of our own, with money made at a job I got on my own and drank my alcoholic drink that came from my fully stocked bar that I didn't swipe from my parents.

Chuckling at myself as I had been supporting myself for a few years already, I took another sip, tucked my bikini bottoms up to expose as much ass cheek to the sun as possible without giving the neighbors something more to talk about and closed my eyes.

Keesha came home shortly after, we had a great routine, I got off at two, she at three and we were generally drunk by four everyday working on our tans and depleting the bar. This afternoon though had future plans. It was Friday as I mentioned, and friends were coming by to join us in our festivities. We were going to the town festival, which like in every small town consists of a Ferris wheel, some twirling, organ displacing fiberglass car ride, cotton candy, a throw the ball/dart/beanbag and win a toy nobody in their right mind would buy, and a Beer Tent. It was held within walking distance from our place.

Though it may not sound like it, I loved living there as it seemed that we were always within walking distance to things. We were central and friends would come to hang out at our place because of it.

I was long past seeing sober by the time we left to go to the beer tent and yet I managed to hold it together in public while we had fun all night. Each taking turns buying rounds, posing for pictures thinking at the time they would look fantastic and upon development just showed me how many drinks I'd had.

That night our apartment was the place where diehards came to finish off the evening. A group of our friends trekked back with us in various states of drunkenness. We sat around laughing, recouping the evening, just chilling out, not wanting the night to be over yet. As all nights do though, this one eventually came to a close and the group began to dwindle.

I took the now more intimate gathering to a new level. At my shit disturbing yet still loveable friend Jerome's direction, this took the form of me plastering my breasts, now exposed from my shirt and covered only by my bra, against Jimmy's face for a photo op that to this day I cannot believe I did. Shortly after, Jimmy and another guy left too.

There were four of us left and it was around two in the morning now.

But it didn't stop there, it was followed up with a shorts swapping event (still being captured on film) with Tig, another one of my good friends', who for the record is male and incidentally Keesha's boyfriend. Don't get too upset, she was the one taking photos as we all laughed hysterically. His shorts were hanging low enough on my hips to see that my thong underwear matched my now famous bra. He couldn't even do up my little shorts, so he just walked around with them open.

When Tig and I exchanged back each others clothes, I got comfortable and changed into a robe and took off the now famous panty set – this would later prove useful. Soon after that Keesha and Tig holed up in her room and it was just me and Jerome left.

One thing lead to another, more drink was consumed, and we moved onto my beloved balcony to leave Keesha and Tig in peace as if they were actually sleeping. Jerome and I joked around, told stupid jokes as one does when drunk and as the night progressed so did the sexual energy.

Flirting was running rampant and proximity to one another was getting closer. It was one of those energies where there are two single people in the same room of opposite sex who are both drunk and horny. It was inescapable in hindsight, without needing to be said, this was going to be a "what happens here stays here" thing, but it was not stopping at flirting. We danced around it, both on the same page and now prolonging the inevitable. Bantering back innuendos and taunting with words what the future held.

I stood there leaning on the rail, my nipples hardening in awareness, certainly not because I was cold as the evening was downright balmy. He sat in the chair in front of me, our eyes playing a game that words were not required for. He reached up, pulled on the bow of my robe. The ties laid loosely on each side, the center gaped open slightly, a hint of the warm body beneath revealed to him. I didn't flinch, it wasn't unexpected it just crossed over from thinking to action.

We continued to stand there having some conversation, my robe agape as if nothing had changed, when everything just had. The not so subtle movement of raising my leg to his chair opened the robe further, keeping some measure of coverage for my pussy yet exposing my torso more, leaving a clear view of the hollow between my breasts right down to my navel. The material catching on my hardened nipples the only thing preventing him full view. His eyes predictably took in what was offered.

He reached up and slid first one hand into the material, the hand caressing my stomach and around to my back as he exposed me slowly, the material grazed as it slid the way of his hands, he repeated the same action on the other side, his eyes remained on mine, neither of us said a word. I stood before him exposed and enjoyed the power I felt in that nudity while he was fully dressed.

I could see the effect it was having on him. I reveled in it. I had to have more. I knelt on my knees, braced my arms on his legs. For all the banter of before there was a silence in that moment. We didn't need words. While my eyes remained on his, I placed my hands on his fly, feeling the ridge beneath. Anxious with anticipation I delayed my progress, waiting for permission that wasn't really needed.

With no negative reaction from him, I pushed further. With both hands I undid his pants and released his confinement marginally. Again I looked up to his eyes, saw encouragement and I reached into his shorts and took his pulsing cock in my hand. I love the feel of a hard cock, such a contradiction, silky yet so hard beneath. I was salivating. I wanted him in my mouth and proceeded to show him how much.

Drawing my tongue around the tip of him, I saw his head lean back to the wall behind the chair and then I closed my eyes and let the need take over. I licked him from base to tip, got him as wet as I was, then continued and took him into my mouth. The feel of him filling my mouth, the heat slid along to the back of my mouth. I wanted to take more but felt the gag reflex kick in. Instead I sucked him, drew him gently in and out of my mouth, my hand held him steady, kept his cock where I wanted it. I glided my hand up and down along his length; I took as much pleasure as I gave. With my eyes still closed in enjoyment I felt his hand rest lightly on my head. His fingers entangled in my hair, I could hear the light moan coming from him. So engrossed in my action I forgot this was for his enjoyment. I opened my eyes and with my hand still engaged with him I watched him.

I knew then though that it wasn't going to be enough for me, screw the consequences that were trying to penetrate my sexual fog. I didn't seem to care that this was a friend of mine, one I would have to face in the morning after having done the nasty with him. I stood up, his eyes followed me. I turned around and he understood what I was about to do, his hands came to my hips, my hands to the chairs arms and we both guided me down unto his lap. Onto his erect cock. He slid in inch by inch, raised and lowered until he was fully inside me and then I stopped. Just for a moment, in bliss, from the pleasure of the feeling of him deep in me. Whether I wanted to stay in that moment or not, my body had other needs.

I ground my hips down then rose up again, a slow undulating action took over, his hands raised to cup my breast and he rolled my nipples in his fingers. My head naturally threw back in pleasure. I could not keep up this slow pace. I needed release. I increased the pace, perspiration glowed on my back, and his hands grasped my hips under the robe that was now a hindrance. That robe was also the only thing that provided any cover from the people that passed by below. I caught the robe in my hands and gathered it to my waist. I watched us having sex. I watched him revealed and disappear inside me. He was so hard; I just slid onto him like a glove. I placed his hand up on my breast, with a need to have the connection all over, I rode him until I was too weak in the legs to do the work and then let him take us the rest of the way required, his hands and arm strength guided my hips.

When we were spent and boneless we somehow made it to my bed, collapsed and fell instantly to sleep. It was a long day, I had been drunk for hours and we had drawn out the foreplay a long time before we got down to it.

I remember being aware of him in my bed. This is where the holy shit factor began to creep in. I have no doubt it did so for him as well because it wasn't two hours later, awake again and sober, he crawled out of the bed, trying not to wake me to presumably head home.

We exchanged the standard smile (albeit awkwardly and without eye contact) and said the 'I'll call you later' bit and he was gone. I went back to sleep and thought; Fuck, I just screwed Jerome.

5

Showers

Everyone has there fetishes, this is one of mine

I was twenty seven when I first discovered my appreciation of 'cool' showers. Meaning showers with some kind of eclectic, interesting, or aesthetic appeal. I'd had sex in the shower before, often with a lack of hand holds, foot holds or places to hoist your ass up onto, not to mention tile chaffing if it got a wee bit aggressive. Cool showers help you forget all that even though it still may be there.

Like any other great sex story, atmosphere adds a great deal to the experience. The first cool shower looked over the ocean by way of one way glass and it was huge, there was a ledge as well. I don't think I could have made a better shower. Of course it was my first cool shower so I was biased.

Since then I find myself asking about bathrooms when reserving hotels and looking at houses and apartments. The cool factor is most assuredly not to be overlooked.

There was the heart shaped one; fun, though too small, the Jacuzzi, erotic and fun with the jet option, hot! There was the stunning tub with a window that opened up to view a gorgeous sunset over the ocean and there was the tub that had louver shutters that opened up to look through the hotel room and out to the mountains. It would have been an excellent place for a good shag had I not been spending the night with three other women I was incidentally not attracted to enough to share my love of cool bathrooms.

I have found that I also prefer bathrooms with windows, preferably with a view. I like to have the option of hot steamy showers or baths with a cool breeze sneaking in. I have been in one of those big claw foot tubs like they always have in the movies, that one wasn't quite big enough for two adults to lounge about in and be super comfortable, but for a little bit it was fun.

Its was a dry, hot day outside, one of those days when you know that even if you go have another dip in the pool, you would still become hot and sticky again within ten minutes. Even so, I went for a dip.

The feel of cool water enveloping my hot body was pure pleasure. A moment where I closed my eyes and nothing existed but that moment. Opening my eyes I slid the rest of my body through the water as I swam across to the other side of the pool, dunking my head and cooling off my whole body.

I then raised myself out of the pool and dropped into a lounge chaise to once again apply sunscreen and get hot and sticky and hopefully add a little colour to my pale Irish freckled skin.

I put my sunglasses back on, picked up my book, and adjusted myself for optimal comfort, made sure my drink was in reach and set myself up to read and suntan.

Out of the corner of my eye I saw him head up in the direction of his room. 'He' was the man I was sleeping with that week. He was wearing his swim trunks, an orange and black pair that reached his knees. It was not an overly revealing outfit though I knew what it concealed. That thought was enough to have me press my knees together and follow his path with my eyes. When he disappeared into the room I waited a moment, when he did not come out immediately I went back to reading my book, watching the door peripherally.

When he still had not come out fifteen minutes later, I started thinking about him maybe up there taking a siesta, mmm maybe he was naked sprawled out on the bed and maybe I could be too.

Of course I got up and started walking up the same path he had. When I got there he was not on the bed as I had envisioned, though he was naked. He saw me, smiled, said he was going to take a shower, and then asked if I wanted to join him

There are some questions that though they are not rhetorical, need not be answered.

I walked into the shower.

When I say that – I mean it. The shower was in the corner of the room, it was a five by five stall with a big glass wall and door making up the entrance side. The two sides that made up the outside corner were only tiled half way from the floor up and then from the little ledge up it had one way glass that gave a panoramic view out over the ocean.

I was still in my bikini as I went into the shower and looked out over our friends as he started the shower adjusting the temperature before we got under any spray.

He came up behind me, pressing into my backside. I could feel him hardening against me. He kissed the hollow of my neck and I was lost.

Turning around and embracing him we began a serious make out session that quickly found me divulged of my bikini top. His head came down to take my breast in his mouth as his hands worked my bottoms down. When he had me gloriously naked and wet he pushed me up against the shower window. I balanced on the tiny ledge spreading my thighs wide as he slid into me in one sleek motion.

We ground against one another, me grasping at hand holds that did not exist, panting and just madly fucking. My head tossed back in a frenzy of rapture, I came. Taking my moans into his own mouth, he came with me.

Feeling like I had actually lost sight of reality for a moment when I came to, I slowly put my legs back down, gingerly testing their ability to hold me up. His wet body was still right with me, sliding against me.

There is something SO sexy about a wet body sliding along my own. Mmm.

I picked up the soap and began to clean him; we shared soaping each other up and being far more thorough than required enjoying each others nooks and crannies. Within no time we were involved in another position, less rushed and with a lot of laughter and fun.

I have never been so clean, nor enjoyed a shower so much.

There was a definite thrill to having sex in that shower while looking down upon my friends below who were enjoying the pool unknowing of the gratifying experience I was indulging in. I wanted to press myself against that one way glass. Undeniably I wanted them to know and ultimately I was glad they didn't, it was like performing without any risk. It was such a turn on. I had sex in that shower on more then one occasion, that's a definite.

6

Women

Oh, the softness that is woman

I have been in varied levels of involvement with a few women. Each of course is beautiful, intelligent, creative and exciting. And each one of them brought something unique to me.

It was not a man who first had me realizing I was a sexy woman, it was a woman, we will call her Lyn. At the time, I had no idea the extent of her feelings and regretfully I did not handle our involvement with the care required. She however was amazing. I mean as bad as it is, when a man says you're hot, nine times out of ten he is thinking about sex. When I woman says another woman is hot, nine times out of ten, she just thinks you're hot. When I was in my work out class last week, a girlfriend who was behind me told me my ass looked great doing squats. I felt complimented, laughed, and said thank you. If a guy friend said it, I would be thinking was he picturing himself slappin' my ass and doin' it doggy style? I am not saying it's fair or valid, but if he's not gay, that is what I think.

As years go by, memories fade, even the ones that maybe should have somehow remained intact out of courtesy. I remember Lyn telling someone I was sexy. That isn't the same as beautiful which I never thought that I was physically. But I was going to take the sexy comment because I knew, even with the insecurities I had, I owned that one. I knew how to work it. Lyn on the other hand was beautiful, I imagine she still is. One of those women with flawless skin that feels like silk, who never looked as if they wore makeup and was always in the right outfit, saying the right thing.

So when Lyn was complimenting me, I took notice and felt pretty damn good about myself. She was the first person I didn't think had anything to gain or wasn't "supposed to" feel that way about me.

As I alluded to above, I suppose I could have been wrong on that one, because Lyn later told me that she'd had feelings for me, unbeknownst to me, for some time. How is it the instinctual flags come up when it's a man, but all the blatant signs coming from a woman and I was blind to them?

I was probably sixteen when I first kissed Lyn. We would go to the bars (yes underage), and if guys bugged us that we were not interested in, I would go make out with her and tell them, 'sorry guys, you're not my type' and leave them to their own conclusions.

I remember one time we were at a club with Rob, we were dancing while Rob stood at the bar. A guy came up to us, I told him he wasn't my type, and he didn't believe me so I made out with her. He said he was cool with that, and asked could he come home with us. I told him sorry we were going home with that guy, and pointed to Rob. Realizing he was on story detail, when the guy went over to him unbelievingly, Rob corroborated my story, acknowledging that yes he was in fact going home with the two of us. It was hilarious, he made it out like, "I know, it's a hard ship but someone has to please these woman' as usual I have gotten off topic, we did not go home with Rob that night or any other night – sorry Rob.

I never realized that it was always me being the one to initiate the make-outs; they happened often enough, I guess I figured we both just did it. Truth is she never instigated it. She pointed this out to me years later when I insisted on having a conversation with her about our relationship one night after a party while I was drunk.

She, rightly so, implied it was incredibly bad timing to have such an important discussion involving her feelings and my surprise over them. To say I fucked that one up would be an understatement that I could write a book on in itself. The next morning after I had indeed convinced her to talk, I woke up realizing I had no idea what we had talked about but I knew I had agreed to do something I was not ready for then, if ever. So I ran. I went to a good friend's house to sort out what was going on. I never discussed it with him, I just needed space. The problem with this; the friends' house I went to was also her ex's.

I was staying with her on weekends, when I got back with some perspective and ready to talk about it, all my stuff was packed up and she wouldn't talk to me. She didn't for probably four years.

When she finally contacted me, I fucked up again!!! With the same guy – I guess some friendships are not meant to be. We have not spoken since, and because it may never happen in person I apologize to her with my whole heart here and now. Not because I wasn't interested in a relationship with her, though I may have flirted and played, I realized then I was not able to be serious about it and she deserved that. I apologize to her for the horrible handling of her feelings at the time.

Prior to all that though, I had a beautiful if ignorant delve into the differences between men and women with her.

What is the difference one may ask? Aside from the obvious physical anatomy, it's the whole package. Women smell different, they touch different, their skin is smoother, their lips softer, they kiss differently, and they connect differently. I will not write here and pretend that all women are the same, of this I am certain however there is this generality that defines why one hetro sexual woman experimenting or one bi-sexual woman could choose a woman over a man on any given moment.

Having been traumatized by my first experience and never wanting to feel responsible for another woman's upset, it took me ten years and an incredible wild woman, otherwise known as bootygirl – yes, the woman who wasn't shy about verbalizing her enjoyment with Billy- to have me letting go of the guilt and giving it another go in the fun and experimental department.

I was not having a good night that night; my substance intake was winning in my battle. I refused to step out of the washroom stall, she stayed with me, holding my hair as I heaved water, consequently also the night I flushed my glasses down the toilet and overflowed the loo at System Sound bar.

My memory is a little fuzzy though I distinctly remember the contrast of her breast and the silky soft skin of her nipple against my tongue and thought, no wonder guys dig this, I didn't want to give it up. I don't remember how it came about (I feel like I say that a lot, I'm not an airhead, I just abused alcohol a lot when I was younger, it's much fewer and far between now) I know I was sitting on the lid of the loo, knowing there was nothing left in my stomach water or otherwise to come out. I hadn't had a drop of alcohol, I had been drinking water all night and hadn't eaten, so the heaving was hurting more then being productive. As I sat there taking a break but not wanting to embarrass myself by leaving my protective 3x5 cell of choice, she stood before me with my water in hand asking me if I was ok.

Next thing I remember her shirt is up and I am touching her. Feeling yourself up is entirely different than someone else. I know when it's coming, to see her reactions.... well I felt like a teenage boy, all aware, eager and enthralled by every little thing.

I know we made out in that stall while her boyfriend danced his ass off in the club.

It was surreal, from nothing to naked breast, mouths and tongues engaged then back to nothing, out in the dance floor like after ten years nothing had changed when it all had. Those same curiosities peaking up again without fear of misunderstanding – I think I explained it all to her that night; she was patient with me, and generous. Here was this women who knew exactly what she wanted from me and it was merely a moment in time in the loo, it wasn't going anywhere beyond what it was. A chance to say its okay little duckling, go spread your wings.

My third brought me further into that realm of freedom, just being able to have fun without attachments. I had thought about her for some time before we hooked up. I had almost had a threesome with her and my then boyfriend one Halloween. I remember him coming up to me and saying she was coming home with us. But that's a different drama. It was not until many months later I found myself at a party and goofing around with her. We ended up getting half naked in the living room while the rest the party was outside skinny dipping. Soon after we were totally naked taking a shower together, I was kissing her against the tiles in the shower (again the shower, there is definitely a pattern).

I went out for my birthday last year with a girlfriend, at the end of the evening there are some snapshots of us giving each other a birthday kiss. It was all in good fun and completely harmless. I have a picture on my wall to remind me of the giggles women can enjoy that are harmless.

Following that, a few months later I went out for another birthday and was completely surprised when the birthday girl planted one on me after telling me I was the coolest and then proceeded to launch into a game of tonsil hockey. I may not have minded so much had I had any inclination it was coming or if she perhaps had asked permission. I am not generally comfortable in the role of superior experience; I have no desire to be the one in the know how. I much prefer the stumble along and giggle level of familiarity.

That said, I enjoyed a few memories with a woman who five years earlier you could not have made me believe for all the money in the world I would end up with her. When we met she was so.. hmmm how to say it, stand offish? It took me a couple years of seeing this woman at events before I felt like I could easily talk with her and another year before we became solid friends. This woman has taught me about loving my body. I have learned how sexy a responsive woman is by watching her. I have felt a level of comfort and trust with her that I never knew. But even with her, we never had sex; we just messed around a lot.

I'm done now I think; I mean I am not opposed to the random make out session with a woman. I have also learned never to say never. I may yet have sex with a woman but I am not out seeking it currently.

7

Morning Sex

Love it!

Perhaps it's subconsciously related to the first time I ever had sex and waking up in the morning only to realize the full ramifications of what I had done in my drunken state the night previously. I now love morning sex because it's a way to confirm I wanted to be with this person. Sounds like good psycho babble, no?

Truth is, if I went to bed with a man, more than likely I was thinking about him in my sleep. I could smell his unique scent all night, I can feel him in the bed with me and I just wake up plain old horny.

Whatever the reason, I do love morning sex. It's right up there in the top three.

Whether it's me or him doing the initiating, doesn't matter to me. If you can rouse me from sleep already having sex with me – all the power to you, as far as I am concerned its one of the best ways to be woken up. Just thinking about it now I am smiling.

I find that everything is heightened in the morning. More intimate, and for me anyways, less hurry up and let's have sex. I save my passionate five minute sex life for the evenings or even mid afternoon. In the morning, it's usually before the alarm goes off – unless I have set it early to purposely give myself time, wink wink.

I am an energetic morning person, but when we are talking about morning sex, I am into the caress and slow flow. Our bodies all warm from sleep, we are not fully conscious and taking the time to feel everything that's happening. Mmm, wish it was morning now and there was a man in my bed.

This next story didn't actually happen physically, this story was written when I was dating a guy who lived in another city. This was what I wrote and sent to him one day when I was thinking about what the morning could look like if he was there with me.

Slowly coming to consciousness I stretched a little and was reminded of my previous evening's activities by the tenderness between my legs. Reaching down I felt my still swollen lips and a wetness, I was ready and wanting some of my much loved morning sex.

With that thought in mind I turned over and let my eyes gaze over the sleeping man in my bed. He looked so peaceful in sleep, his gorgeous green eyes hidden behind his lids, eyes that told me so much, a day's growth of beard on his face giving credence to the man that he was. A passionate man, one who knew how to please a woman. I smiled at that thought, he was a phenomenal lover. I squeezed my legs together to stem the need rising within while I continued to look at him.

The sheet was haphazardly draped across his midsection, baring the chest I could enjoy touching for hours. His light sprinkling of hair that I loved to run my hands in, while it tickled between my fingers. Following the trail down further I moved the sheet to take in his whole body. His legs were so strong. He had an ass that jeans were made for and his heritage lent him year round color to his skin. Then I allowed myself to look at the part of him that could bring me to orgasm in seconds. Even in sleep he was impressive.

Longing to touch him, to bring us both to that passionate place we found so easily together. Our chemistry so potent it blew my mind, leaving me speechless for minutes on end.

Just thinking about it had my mouth going dry and pulse racing in anticipation. Rubbing my legs together, I reached back down between my legs and touched myself. Wanting to relieve some of the pressure so that I could enjoy more than a quickie with this man I could happily spend the day in bed with when our lives would permit it.

'Mmmm' comes to mind when I think of all the ways we had made love, the creative places found when we couldn't wait to have sex with one another, the hot and blatant fucking we often did when passion got in the way of finesse.

My pelvis automatically thrust in response to the thoughts and my fingers offered little of the satisfaction I was craving.

I wanted him inside me, thrusting in and out. He could get so hard, so thick; I could feel his cock sliding along my entrance and all inside me. He touched everywhere. Damn, I could almost orgasm just at the images of those memories.

He truly had a beautiful cock, all smooth and silk over a shaft that could get so hard it was like steel. His balls were perfectly proportioned and he kept himself trim. If I didn't feel like I should bring him to a peak relatively soon after I began to touch him I could caress him and mold him and lick him and play with him for days.

Itching to touch him now, I reached out and caressed his face, trailed my hand along that rough stubble, just imagining that same light scratch as if it were along my thigh. I was torturing myself. I continued to caress down his chest, past the dip between his pecks stopping briefly to play. He began to stir a little as he became aware of my ministrations.

Following the path I started, I grazed down and across his thighs. He rolled to his back and his legs fell more open, allowing me the access I wanted. How accommodating of him, I smiled and wondered just how conscious he was now. Twirling circles around his upper and inner thighs I could hear his breathing change slightly. I angled myself up and over his chest and while my right hand rose to cup his balls, I leaned down and with the tip of my tongue teased his nipple. A tight intake a breath was my reward as his hand came up to tangle in my hair and massage my scalp in encouragement.

I took his cock in my hand, gliding slowly up and down with light pressure, a tease almost but it was with definite appreciation as he began to grow in my hand. My hand pressure strengthened as he did and I began to trail a combination of kisses and licks along his neck, leading up to his ear, taking his lobe in my teeth and lightly nibbling while allowing my breath to hit his sensitive inner ear. Sliding the tip only of my tongue lightly around the shell of his ear and blowing softly on the wetness left behind causing a shiver to come from him and a smile to his lips.

I leaned down and gently pressed my lips to his chin, he turned seekingly towards my lips but I evaded them and continued to kiss his forehead, his eyelids his cheeks his nose and then finally returning to kiss the corner of his mouth.

This time when he turned into me, I allowed a light kiss. Slipping my tongue out I lightly licked along the seam of his lips, he responded by licking his own lips. His other hand came up to grasp my head in both his hands and bring my face and lips down to exactly where he wanted me.

As the kisses became more passionate my hand became more insistent as well.

His tongue slid in and around my mouth, and I was reminded of his tongues talents elsewhere on my body. His kisses were intoxicating, bringing such pleasure to me. I swore at times this mans lips were made to pleasure me alone. His lips were so soft, they gave the perfect amount of give, and he used his tongue just right, licking and sliding without ever being too wet. God he was amazing, I was so turned on.

Wanting to get him to the same place as me, I pulled away from those God given glorious lips and moved myself down his body to share with him my own talents. My lips soon joining the hands that had been attending him, I took his cock in my hand and positioned it for my mouth to receive him and licked the tip of his cock.

Again another indrawn breath between clenched teeth. I then licked him from base to tip laving him all over while still sliding him in my hand. I took his cock in my mouth and sucked him. Rolling my tongue around him in my mouth. Loving the feel, and taste of him.

Now awake and fully conscious he was up on his elbows looking down at the pleasure I was giving him, I could tell he was enjoying the wet heat and pressure I was providing for him.

It was not long before he took my hips in his hands and maneuvered me so that I was straddled over him with my head down on him and my own heat positioned in front of his face. I loved the joint pleasure I knew he was about to begin though it distracted me as well from what I was doing.

Without hesitation or preamble he grabbed my ass, his hands spreading me open before him and took me into his mouth all wet heat, his thick tongue licking me and feasting on my clit. He suckled me gently. His tongue doing a combination of light nibbles and a rhythmic rubbing of my most sensitive spot. God I wanted to continue to give him pleasure as well but he was robbing me of coherent thought. Reveling in the divine pleasure of his capable and gifted mouth.

Just when I thought I had gained enough control over my arousal he slipped a finger into my wetness, sliding it along my lips and then right into me taking my breath away, I could not contain the moan that escaped me if I'd tried to.

With new inspiration I took him back into my mouth and gave him equal pleasure. Pumping his moistened cock up and down with my hand, cupping his balls and massaging them while I greedily took as much as I could into my mouth, laving and sucking him.

As I was sure I was about to orgasm and knowing he was close as well he push me forward causing me to lean down still on my knees but my hips remaining raised he pulled himself out from under me. He changed our positions so that he was now behind and over me, hips in hand, in one clean thrust he was inside me. He thrust powerfully and deeply into me, in long sure strokes.

Crying out in ecstasy, I moved my hips in tandem with his thrusts and in no time I was arching my back in the throws of an immensely powerful orgasm. My spasming inner walls clenching and milking him to his own release. As a guttural moan came from him he bent over me and I turned my face to connect with him, our lips fusing as the potent orgasm took us both over the edge leaving us weak and mindless.

I eased myself down taking him with me and enjoyed the heat and weight of him on top of me as our body's energy began to restore itself in slow increments. I could feel his heart erratically pulsing as was my own.

Slowly as our heart beats worked their way to a more regular rhythm and our slick bodies cooled, he shifted, taking me with him into a spoon position and while still inside me, we both fell back into a deeply satisfied and blissful slumber.

8

Rompolicious

Sometimes you just need to create new words

I walked down the street with my friend Geoff and as we chatted the conversation turned to sex – not uncommon around me. I told him that I had had sex that was so amazing that the man I was with created a new word to describe it, as no other fit.

I told Geoff I would only share the word if he promised that he would only use it himself if he found himself in intimate relations that were beyond anything he had ever experienced. Loving that left him speechless well past the time it took him to regain something resembling normal breath and had retrieved his eyeballs from the back of his head where they had rotated to in ecstasy and could not easily find their way right again.

A moment when he could look at his woman and could seriously not believe humans were capable of such intense emotion and bliss and created magic. Positively euphoric, incredibly enlightened, off the charts, word steeling, breath taking, bone melting, immobilizing, a whole body encompassing orgasmic experience.

Welcome to Rompolicious.

It was a one of those perfect summer days that cottages are sought after for. It was mid summer, the lake had heated up enough that even I would go in it, the beer was cold, the group of friends gathered were cool, music was playing and we were all enjoying a great weekend.

I had come into the bedroom to give my freckles a break from the sun and cool off, to have a nap – I love napping and think more people should do it. It was mid-afternoon; it was hot and humid outside. I was mildly buzzing from the couple of drinks I had already had. With the curtains closed, keeping the sun from blazing in the room I knew the sheets would be an inviting temperature. I peeled back the top sheet and removed my clothes intending to slide into the bliss; crisp sheets in the hot summer.

Before I could slip in and give over to the nap that was calling, he came into the room to get out of his wet swim trunks. It was a time in our relationship when the sex was great and often. When I saw him, my nap was immediately put on the back burner and I wanted to sneak a quickie before he went back out to join our friends.

Whether it was his intention as well or not, I don't know, but we were often in sync. As I stood there watching him, letting my intentions be known he dropped his shorts, I could see the instant arousal we caused for each other. His dick proudly springing to attention, my nipples hardening and craving his touch. Without further ado we began making out both with a one track mind.

There was honestly nothing special about the timing, the room, or anything else you could think of. I had been in the sun all day, was not at my most fresh, smelling of sunscreen, lake water and likely a little sweat, same with him, you could even add in a that we likely both tasted of beer.

Wrapped up in each other and moving as one, we made our way to the bed and fell upon it, limbs all over one another, hands in each others hair and all over each others sun warmed bodies wherever we could reach

We quickly lost all concept of where we were, that our friends were just outside, we were so caught up in each other.

I think right from the beginning somehow it was different; I just did not recognize it then. It was spontaneous, sensual, sexy, hot and playful all at the same time.

We kissed slower, my eyes closing, his lips meeting mine with the lightest of touch, the softness of his lips grazing mine, nipping, sliding back and forth. His tongue slipped out and provided moisture, allowing the kisses to glide. I have read books that reference a kiss that mimics making love. I had always had difficulty visualizing that, I don't now.

These kisses were everything you want when making love, it was a promise, it told me we were both fully present in this moment, it told me he loved me, it told me he thought I was sexy, it told me how much he wanted me, and it told me how our making love was going to be.

It was erotic, slow, and moist. It was teasing, it was giving and receiving, it was gentle and intoxicating. It was sexy, slow and yet passionate and fun. That summer we really loved one another and it came across in whatever we did.

Our hands gliding over one another, exploring bodies we already knew so well as if we had never touched before, giving the attention of one who is excited about what they are discovering. Caressing, yet with fingertips pressing in, acknowledging the building passion, the energy rising in both of us.

As our legs entwined, rubbing along one another, toes trailing up legs, thighs caressing thighs, sliding back and forth emulating the dance that was yet to begin.

I could feel him further hardening and growing against me, an answering wetness between my thighs wanting him inside me right then and yet wanting to have this pleasure as well. I knew when I took him inside me I would lose my ability to hold onto this sweet exploring tone.

My hands trailing his back, across the width of his shoulders and up into his hair. Running my fingers in his hair grazing his scalp with my nails all the while our lips still loving one another. My breast pressed up against his chest. My nipples going from soft and silken to budding and firm. He reached up to cup my breast with his hand, enclosing, lifting and caressing me, then taking my nipple into his mouth. Licking around its hardened tip and then slowly sucking on it. I could feel the pull down my stomach and between my legs, reacting by squeezing my thighs around his leg that was raised up between mine. As I raised my outer leg higher around his hip, he slipped inside me.

It was not one of those eager and immediate sessions where you cannot wait to get past the urgency. I looked at him, and with our eyes locked I think then we both knew this one was different. He, gliding in and out of me, I could feel every inch of him and every inch of me where he was and then wasn't. My body so sensitive, our bodies slowly heating, creating that sheen of sweat that is so hot I could not help but run my hands all over him and him me.

I could smell us, the smell of sex, and of our own scents combining. It was so erotic. So sensual.

I had no desire for this to be over, I wanted it to go on forever.

I love sweaty sex, no, let me clarify that, I really love sweaty sex with this man, I love everything about him. His wet body, the result of our loving was such a turn on and I wanted to please him. After we had rolled around in various positions probably too many to review, I crawled on top. With him deep inside me I rocked on him, grinding my hips into him, feeling him everywhere and every which way I could within me.

I rode him, sliding back and forth on him at varied speeds, getting us both feeling fucking incredible and working up that sheen of perspiration all over me. I love it when I am so into it that I get sweaty and can run my hands easily along my body. I stroked myself, and lifted my breasts while I rode him, taking care of business.

I rotated around, fuck did it feel good. I knew he liked my ass so that's what he saw. His hands on me gently guiding yet letting me do my thing. I was so into it. What was probably only minutes felt like hours as I enjoyed him and us. I used his legs as a hand hold to just go to town and go as fast as I could, the pressure building within me. Part of me wanting to stop to prolong the feeling of him inside me and part of me just wanting to let loose on him, get him off while I was on top which I rarely do.

Backwards, forwards, looking him in the eye as I did my best to give us pleasure. His hands coming up to cup my breasts, sliding along my torso, pinching my nipples, at times I could tell he was not even seeking to give me pleasure he was just grasping in response to what was going on within himself, such incentive to continue.

Licking my lips, ignoring the burn in my legs, knowing this was beyond what I had given before, I loved him, and I gave him everything I had. Taking him deep, riding just the tip of him, letting him feel everything that was going on inside me in action over words.

There were a lot of smiles exchanged, there were moans, groans and a lot of heat. As I got more wet and he seemingly got harder if that's possible, I slid and I grinded. There were many sheet grabbing moments, a lot of moaning, hip gyrating, sweat inducing, fondling, exploring, discovering moments. There was a lot of eye contact and silent communication mixed in with some potent kisses that I didn't want to stop, multiple peaks culminating in the most intensely powerful, thought stopping, word stealing, blinding orgasm I had ever had. Completely collapsing, my seemingly boneless body draped onto his.

About ten minutes after, we both lay on our backs, chests still rising and falling deeply, we turned to one another, without the words that I could not have said anyway we acknowledged what happened as being like nothing we had ever experienced. Licking my lips and attempting to regain the ability to think in communicable sentences. I trailed my hand down my torso still tingling with all the aftereffects of the experience.

There was love in both our eyes and wonderment for me as he reached up to cup my face in his hand and kissed me lightly, his tongue slipping out to just lick my lips. My body was still so involved it was like he licked my core, it shot right threw me and I knew I might never experience that again, and would never be able to give an accurate description of what happened within me.

As the years pass, some of the little details have become vague and the order of details mixed up, though I very clearly remember the eye contact, the knowing looks and that look we exchanged at the end, I still remember the feeling that came over me. My whole body, my mind, that day I made love with my soul and touched the heavens.

9

My First Time

Memorable for the wrong reasons

We can, and will talk about the literal first time in a moment. But before that, let's just talk about the man I was with after him. The one with whom I made a clear choice and decided to sleep with, and yes I will clear up why that is relevant. This was a guy who I dated for almost a year. We didn't wait that long, more like a month maybe- I was just establishing it was a boyfriend relationship. If I remember correctly, our first date was on Valentines Day, ahhhh. He had a massive cock, and sometimes I feared it. I was also pretty new to sex and he was a few years older and much more experienced. I could write about how I laid there, not knowing anything about what I liked yet. I mean after a bit it got better for sure but I was still learning.

I remember that first time with him thinking why does anyone like sex, this just hurts. I thought it wasn't supposed to hurt after the hymen's been broken? As I laid there thinking these thoughts, wondering how long it was going to last, something began to shift, the pain was easing and something else was happening, it was starting to feel pretty damn good. This little butterfly was fluttering around in me. And as he started to kiss me again now that he was fully embedded inside me I got wrapped up in that and allowed myself just to feel it all.

Then I had my first orgasm, I was shocked, embarrassed, elated, giddy, naïve and it was beautiful. I wanted to do it again, but was too tender. We had a fairly regular sex life I think, depending on what you quantify as regular. We didn't live together but we had sex whenever we saw one another. He kissed like a dream, now many years later I think blindfolded I could still pick him out if he kissed me.

But, back to the real first time story. ..

It was December, and a group of us were all hanging out together at our friend Mike's place. This was not unusual, most weekends the "gang" could be found at one of our parents' homes or the other. This weekend we had come up to Mikes, we were checking out his new house, he now lived closer to all of us. We hung out in the basement drinking and having a little pre Christmas cheer. It was harmless and contained good old teenage fun. There were at least six of us there, six I remember that play into this story anyways.

Some of the guys had exchanged gifts. Dave had gotten the guys each a bottle of Whiskey, I want to say it was 'Teachers' a Brand I had never heard of. As the night wore on someone's bottle was opened on top of the alcohol we had purchased that evening. I would say we were all loaded. My girlfriend Mac was drinking Blue Lagoons, I say this now because later its funny. I don't recall what I was drinking, only that I progressively got chatty, a sign I am done for.

I remember having a conversation for about two hours with Steve and Dave about my virginity. At least it felt like that long but was likely just a long conversation with that topic at the end of it. I remember telling them that I always figured I would do it with Peter; a guy who had been my boyfriend when I was thirteen and still whom I still had enough of affection for, to give him my cherry. I was going on about how I wanted the first time to be with someone I cared about. Since I wasn't one of those girls who always had a boyfriend, it didn't occur to me that it would necessarily be a boyfriend. That's why I thought Peter. We had a history, I trusted him and he was special. I was one of the last virgins I knew, and I figured I was going to give it up soon, little did I know how soon.

It didn't end up happening with Peter, poor guy, never got the honor it could have been. I wouldn't say how I gave it was honorable at all, embarrassing-yes!

All that talk was just completely thrown out the open door less then an hour later. I was both drunk and tired. I knew that I was just not going to be able to stay awake much less drink for much longer. It was late; we were all sleeping over so I asked Mike where I could crash. He walked me upstairs.

There are a couple points to get in before I continue, just to round out the story and not have to backtrack into explanations later. At this point, Mac was puking up blue in the toilet after having begun her hurl fest outside. In the morning the blue puke off to the side of the front walk was just funny rather then disgusting as puke usually is. Blue Curacao mixed with puke is kind of florescent. Anyway, I tell you this because a girlfriend usually has your back where a guy friend has his guy friends back. I have no idea if the guys downstairs knew what was in store or not, but I know if Mac had not been hugging the John, I would have not been hugging Mike.

He showed me into a room I assumed was his, it didn't look neat enough to be a guest room, and who offers up someone else's room. Anyway, one minute we are standing and next I remember we are chatting on the single bed horizontally. Then we were making out, which leads me to the other point to mention. A few weeks before over at Jay's house (this is when Mac and Jay were still dating), Mike and I had a conversation, it's weird but I even remember the song that was playing in the background #7- Sacrifice from Elton John's 'Sleeping with the Past' Album. It was an album that we played often and this song in particular had been on repeat more then once. I think somehow on that night it was the prophecy warning me, obviously I didn't pay attention.

As usual, I digress I am amazed I can find my way back to my point sometimes. We were having a conversation about "us" not that there was an "us", that was the point, he asked if I would like to go out sometime and I said I just wasn't interested in him that way, and enjoyed the dynamic we had as friends. I don't remember why we were alone in the basement, and yet were we for the half an hour plus this conversation lasted. I believe it was after that, I proceeded to do seven vodka shots with a sip of OJ chasers. That night I was very sick, it was YEARS after before I would ever touch vodka, and even a few before orange juice didn't remind me of it. They say you cannot taste vodka, I disagree, when you have been sick on it, it has a tendency to leave an impression.

I fell asleep in front of the fire the night of our conversation and woke up the next morning stiff and freezing and immensely hung over. I still clearly remembered telling Mike I was not interested. I know at the time I thought that he took it really well, casual, like it was nothing. Maybe he figured he would try again later, maybe he WAS ok with it, not a big deal? Who knows, but I'd say I won that round, he won the next.

So now back to the 'first time' story, with that conversation having happened only a couple weeks before you may be puzzled as to how we ended up making out on the bed, especially after I had just been talking about Peter, and Mike had clearly been told only recently he wasn't the one for me. Well, I wasn't coherent enough to be puzzled as you are. I was going with the flow I guess, too drunk to see how contradictory my actions were from my words.

In that moment though, lying on that bed making out; I also knew I was about to have sex. I knew this was not just a little make out party. I know I knew because I am the one who brought up the lack of a condom. Apparently I was not so drunk that I would forget to remember safety. He left the room and went God knew where and was back in a flash. Too short a time for me to contemplate or comprehend how doing this would leave me feeling soon after. Before I gathered my intelligence from the bottle that drowned it, he was there with a look of eagerness which I guess I took to mean he was successful in his errand. We got the appropriate clothing off and with the weirdest feeling; I likely cannot articulate to you, I knew exactly what it was going to feel like before it happened. Things all kind of happened in slow motion, or as if I was not really there but sitting beside me watching it. My body felt everything, but my mind was so completely unengaged in what was happening. I wasn't surprised about any of it, I felt one step ahead of each thing that happened, like it was all a play I had seen, and knew the actions coming up next. I wasn't in pain; there was the expected moment of discomfort but nothing like I thought it was going to be, more awkward than pain. From there it was just happening until I started thinking, hmm when did he put the condom on? So I asked him.

He paused and with a stammered "uhhh, I couldn't find one.." it was over. I told him to get off me, shoved him off and we were done. I wasn't tired anymore, I was a little stunned. I got up, got dressed and went back downstairs and poured myself another drink. Dave and Steve sat there with what I determined to be smirks on their faces. I ignored it for fear that they were smirking about what I didn't want to talk about or acknowledge. I hadn't sorted it out in my own head yet; I sure as hell didn't want to reveal what I was feeling or hear them remind me of what I had said less then an hour before. In no way shape or form was I coerced into it, I know that. I accept full responsibility for it, that doesn't mean though that I wasn't beside myself with confusion on how I let it happen. There they were, looking at me. They knew, I don't know how they knew and, I knew that they knew.

The next morning everyone eventually awoke, we gathered around the table for a family style brunch. And by family, I mean with his parents included, his Mom was making us breakfast. I have no idea when they got home but there we all were. In my ignorance I had no idea the mortification I should have been feeling at that table.

Three weeks later, Mac came storming into my bedroom, shuts my door and in the process of shoving me onto my bed verbally attacks me "Why didn't you tell me, I cannot believe you didn't fuckin tell me?"

"What the hell are you talking about? I asked completely taken off guard, my mind was scrambling for anything that could produce this reaction from her that I had done that day. I came up with nothing since this was the first I had seen her.

"Mike!" one word! Knowing that it was enough, she didn't need to elaborate at all she just stood there bent over me, hands on hips starring and waiting for an explanation.

With fear having drained all the color from my face I tried to buy time and think of something I could tell her – I am a horrible liar but I prayed she didn't actually know, that I was overreacting out of guilt. I meekly respond with 'What about him?"

"YOU SLEPT WITH HIM!" with a combination of still being in shock, unbelievingly hoping for an alternate explanation and hurt, her eyes never wavered from my face even though I could barely look at her.

"How do YOU KNOW THAT?' my voice escalated to a squeak, as once again my brain was off and running with scenarios on how she could have found out, I mean why would Mike have told her when we didn't even finish it?

"Because" she said, like I was dumb, and took a breath before slowly continuing so I would understand, while her chest rose and fell still with emotion "There was no fucking door on his brother's room"

Completely oblivious I asked again what she was talking about, she had confused me.

"On the room you had sex in; there was no DOOR! EVERYONE SAW YOU and Mike having sex!"

If I had not already been on my bed I would have fallen. I sat there with my mouth agape for a moment but it felt like forever as mortification set in, no door, not his room, everyone.....images ran past my eyes as I made the effort to sit up.

"w-what?" Scarcely able to even get that word out, it couldn't be true. I needed to get a handle on what she was saying and what else it could mean. I looked up at her questioningly, my eyes imploring her to provide me a different answer than she had.

'Yeah,' her tone now less angry seeing how staggered and dismayed I was from this news, it was too much to process at once. "Everyone saw, except for me because I was passed out in the bathroom. Everyone knows. His parents saw you for Christ's sake!"

"WHAT?" aghast, that tidbit had got a fresh horrified reaction out of me, my eyes looking at her beseechingly hoping for some of this to be meant as torture for keeping it from her even though I knew she wouldn't be that cruel my brain was just not firing properly right then.

"Why did I learn from someone else?' she asked, the hurt of not knowing now evident. 'They were talking about it like I knew. Why didn't you tell me?" she asked again now with more control.

Devastated I told her the truth "I didn't want anyone to know, so I didn't tell, I thought if I didn't tell I could pretend it didn't happen I guess."

"Well TOO Bad, cause EVERYONE knows!" her frustration back in full force at my ignorance and stupidity. She then plopped herself on my bed with me, gave me a hug, probably a shake and I told her the whole story.

I know everyone has "their first" story, but I do believe that mine is particularly entertaining even if at the time it didn't feel that way for me. Mike never did ask me out again, we did however remained friends after that. Eventually we even would joke about it. My other friends all laughed at me for awhile after they found out I knew they all knew. They would raze me about it like teenagers do to each other. Then we all kind of just got past it, the sting of it lost its power. It just became a story to tell. I think I even told Peter the story of that night.

10

Brazilians

Why do we do this again?

Gentlemen – you may not want to read this chapter though I do believe it will give you a completely different respect for women and what they do in the name of grooming.

I don't remember how old I was when I went for my first bikini wax but I remember the place, 'Tip Top Wax' at the Mall. It was this little place with all European women, like I thought that would make it better somehow. European women in my experience are either totally well kept, or totally not. I thought since these women were the beautifully kept looking ones that they would be so used to it and would know how to make it not hurt. Yeah, it's just never going to be that way, its hair being ripped out! I don't think I went back there, as if a different place could produce better results? I had to try and find a place that the women at least talked to me rather than treating me like a stupid Irish girl who knew nothing of grooming and would never be perfect like them. Attitude affects pain!

I remember one of my girlfriends going for her first wax, she was up visiting on vacation and came to my new place, "the Village Spa", she practically screamed, didn't get more than a tiny strip off each side and that was only to be symmetrical, she had to be convinced into that second side. When my regular esthetician came out of the room, she was laughing.

I could potentially dredge up a funny story or two about waxing from the years in between a regular bikini wax and my first Brazilian for which I could tell you the date and possibly the hour. Instead I will leave you with this bit of advice; MOST women turn red after a wax, its trauma to the body! If you are waxing for an occasion, do it at least a day in advance. I was totally embarrassed once when my boyfriend came over, threw up my skirt to have sex and there I was with big red bald spots. Not the look I was going for.

I swear to you, I never thought I could do a Brazilian. I remember knowing about them, I remember my roommate's boyfriend telling us he would pay for us both to get it done and I thought, he can say that because I will never put myself through that much pain. It's a safe offer. I remember thinking; why the fuck would anyone in their right mind, go through that?

We as women already do so much that most straight men, I truly believe, can never relate to. What's worse is that for the most part, we do it just to please and attract our partners. I swore I wouldn't do it.

Then I moved to Vancouver, not to say that was the reason I changed my declaration but that just happens to be when I did it. I had a friend T (I am not shortening her name for privacy, that's what I called her) who got them regularly. I listened to her say enough times "I'm going to get my Brazilian today" and then another girlfriend Betty -who I didn't think would get one, started getting them as well. On top of that, I was working in a Spa that did them. I began to think hmmm maybe one day. I like to think I will try everything once so I put it in the possibility zone.

T, who so courageously got them all the time, shortly there after moved to the East Coast and I still had not gotten one. My 'back up' encouragement Betty, would tell me they weren't so bad. The more I considered it, I thought it's not a lot more then I am waxing already. I was likely blowing it out of proportion.

I made an appointment. I think I went in having taken some form of Tylenol to potentially combat the excruciating pain I was expecting, irrelevant of what she said. I have a very low pain tolerance when it comes to some things and sure enough I was not to be disappointed. I don't care what they say; Tylenol does NOT work on that kind of pain. Its like, "oh, you've ripped your arm open, let me put a band aid on that gaping wound" does that give you an idea?

I live by a mantra 'to think is to create', so MAYBE I created this pain, though more possibly that's bullshit, it's unnatural and it just fucking hurt!

I have never felt pain like that, granted, I have never given birth, though it seems absolutely ludicrous when doing it, that it will be worth it.

My first time I could not even get it all done, I left there with little patches missed. The esthetician said to me, looking very serious 'you must promise to come back and get another one, do not let this be your only experience of it.' She promised that it would be better next time, the first time is always the worst, she said. I remember thinking as I got dressed that she was into sadism.

Gathering back my pride from where I left it (with my leg wrapped around my head, fully exposing myself to this women in a position I cannot see myself ever offering to a man) I fake smiled, told her I would come back after my trip and left. I walked down the street looking like I just rode a cow. Attempting to give my now angry pink, swollen mostly hair free labia some room, so as not to be traumatized any further by the friction of my pants rubbing against my panties.

Then as I walked down the street on my way to work I noticed something different. I had to call one of the woman I worked with at the Spa; (I didn't have it done where I worked only because I felt odd having coworkers know what I looked like down there, I needed a stranger I didn't have to see again for my first) I told her I had just had my first Brazilian. She asked how I felt; she said she loved having no hair there. I was passing a construction zone at this point, on my cell phone and oddly felt no need to lower my voice, I was now excited and didn't care who knew what I just did. I was liberated. I told her I was tingling. I told her I felt more aware of myself than I ever had. The friction I was feeling as I walked, my 90% hair free labia were sliding along each other in there after wax lotion glory, I swear to you I could have cum while walking.

I knew then, not five minutes after having felt pain like I had never felt, I was truly a masochist; that I would indeed be back. If I felt this aware of myself and still it wasn't all gone, how mind blowing was it going to feel next time.

I took my tingling swollen angry pink yet happy puss to work. I sat gingerly all day with a big smile on my face and knew I was a convert

I went away on my trip and though I did not have sex that first time, I was greatly looking forward to it.

I came back home, I made another appointment, the esthetician I had gone to was not available and although I could not imagine spreading my legs that intimately for yet another woman, I did. She was correct, this time it was easier, it still hurt, that's not going to miraculously go away, though it hurt less and was faster.

The first guy who got to experience my Brazilian could have cared less, he just didn't appreciate things like that, but I did!

I tell you, if you have never touched yourself, never been a woman who knows what her vagina looks like – you will after a Brazilian. These estheticians have you hold yourself here and there pulling the skin tight, moving bits out of the way – it's completely personal. I know that I had never been that open about touching myself in front of a partner, I am much more comfortable about it now.

Back on track, my second experience brought forth new embarrassments.

My girlfriend Loryn has become an esthetician. I think she has found her calling. Mix someone who will say anything combined with someone who does Brazilian waxing and you get statements like I mentioned previously 'you never know when you are going to meet an ass licker.' Perhaps if she had said that to me before my second visit, I would have been prepared.

My second visit, the esthetician said 'turn over'. I thought 'umm, why would I need to do that?' She very casually said

'To do the other side'. Still wary I complied, after rolling over she then had me place one hand on either ass cheek and she said 'spread em'. I cannot tell you how odd that was. She then put hot wax on the crack of my ass down to the opening of my vagina, rubbed in a wax strip and ripped it off. This brings new definition to the concept of ass clenching. 'Oh careful', she said 'I am not done, you will stick together'. "WHAAATT?' I screeched, as I attempted to turn around in astonishment while still holding my ass apart to avoid this sticking when all I wanted to do was escape this indignity. 'T' had mentioned something about being on all fours, I thought she had been kidding; after all it hadn't happened the first time.

I was not blessed as some are with a body that has next to no hair. That said, much of it is like a little blond fuzzy coating 'my peach fuzz'. I had NO idea what a difference removing peach fuzz could make.

Next time I went into the shower and was rinsing off my hand was slipping and sliding like it never had before. I could happily caress my own smooth parts that truthfully I never knew could feel this way before. I was so excited to go have sex and see how other things slid around.

My girlfriend had told me it would rock my world. She was right. There is nothing to get in the way, natural lubricant has no where to hide, you feel everything so much more. And I mean everything. Having a guy give you some sugarpuss after a Brazilian wax, WOW! Here's an exercise to try, or at least visualize, think about what it would be like to lick the backside of a guy's hairy arm, not overly appealing, but now take your tongue and lightly lick the inside bend of your elbow joint. I don't think anymore needs to be said.

My name is Tyler, I am a single white female, and I am thirty years old. It seems to me that losing ones virginity happens younger and younger these days. I was seventeen when I gave mine away at a Party. Since then, I have been no angel. I have had good sex, the kind where you both get off, roll over happy and go to sleep. I have had great sex, where time stands still and you don't remember how to form words let alone breath normally, and I have had bad sex, where no ones happy, no one broke a sweat and frustration takes on new meaning. All this is different from oral sex.

My understanding of Tantric sex is that it is about not having an end goal per say, but to focus on the present, about enjoying each moment. This is an art form to be practiced, cultivated. Well if one goes into the act of Oral like this, then it too can be an art form.

Dave does this for me. He LOVES performing oral sex; he would do it all day long if I would let him. He loves it more than sex. I did not share his love until he suggested I go get waxed. So I went. The next day I got home, Dave and I had a nice dinner and then he suggested I go relax in a bath, he would clean up. Not one to argue with that kind of offer, I went to draw myself a bath. While the water ran, I decided I would fully relax. I got the book I hadn't had time to read, my favorite robe, pinned my hair up and then went and slipped into the sudsy water. I read for a good twenty minutes until the bubbles were dissipating. Then I enjoyed a loofa exfoliation and shaved my legs. I was feeling silky all over. As I was cleaning myself I of course came across my newly hair free juncture, my hands of their own volition gravitating there repeatedly. I could feel myself getting excited, my nipples peaking above the water level, the water lapping against my breasts like a caress. I closed my eyes and enjoyed this new territory. I could feel so much more than I could before. It was so much more sensitive.

I knew I could pleasure myself easily in this moment, but why, when there was a perfectly great specimen in my house. I got out of the tub, slipped on my robe, checked that I didn't have mascara running down my face and went to seek out Dave.

He had been a busy man while I was relaxing. Candles were lit all over the place, a saucy jazz was playing softly and Dave was standing there waiting for me with a glass of champagne and he was naked. Naked and hard I might add. Damn, I wanted this man now. I wanted to have him slide right into me; I was so wet the juices were practically running down my legs.

He stretched out his hand holding the glass, I accepted it. I proceeded to down the entire flute. I have a great bear skin rug in front of the fireplace, cheesy perhaps but in that moment I knew we were going to live out all the cliché fantasy scenes on it tonight. Dave had set up a bunch of pillows by the fire. He couldn't have done this better if a woman had directed him.

I put the glass down and walked to the pillows and sat down, I held my hand up to him, encouraging him to join me. He did. I went to take off my robe but he stopped me. Looked me in the eyes and then leaned in to kiss me.

We have been together long enough that I thought I knew all his kiss types, but this was different. Maybe my mind was playing tricks but it was like he was making love to my mouth. It was slow, it was wet, his tongue was flicking, and he was taking little nips at me followed with small swipes of his tongue, and again little licks.

There was such pressure building I needed his hands on me; truthfully I needed his fingers at least if not his dick in me. I placed his hand on my pussy to show him. He leaned me back onto the pillows and began to trail kisses down my torso, spreading the robe only enough for his task as he went.

I knew what he was going to do; I knew it because he loves to. I knew I wanted more but was not unhappy with the detour.

I don't know if I mentioned it, but I went Full Brazilian. I did not leave a 'landing strip' usually I know where he is if I am not looking because I feel him get to my pubic hair. This time he was at my clit before I knew what hit me. I nearly jumped out of my skin in surprise; the only thing stopping me was his hand on my stomach holding me there.

When I calmed, sheepishly apologizing he began to kiss around where I now wanted him. He kissed the hollow where my hips joins my leg, moving my legs wherever he wanted he kissed and flicked little licks at me so close but not where I wanted it. I could feel my juices seeping out of me, I was so hot and bothered by the feeling of it sliding down to my ass I could barely contain my eagerness. My thighs actually began to tremble.

Seeing this, he shifted himself more securely between my legs and looking up at me once, he then bent his head and blew my mind.

From the first swipe of his tongue, he went bottom to top licking the spilt juices and ending at the tip of my clit. It was the longest lick, the space once a couple centimeters now felt a mile. So many sensations all at once I could not do anything other then gasp out, my fingers clutching for something I couldn't even define. Holy Shit it has never been like this and it's only one lick.

He did it again, this time his fingers gently opened me up to further assault my senses. The air hitting the wet insides, his fingers even on the labia were all things I had not felt before. While his tongue continued to stroke and lick, his fingers crept in. Taking the wetness and gliding around up to my clit but shy of the pressure I needed to relieve, then down to my asshole where he drew circles and then slide up the back side, there was nothing to stop him, it was like I was plastic, no texture there, and yet SO much feeling. I had no idea little hairs had hid so much pleasure from me. We were less then a minute in and I was in ecstasy. I wasn't even thinking about sex anymore. I just wanted him to never stop.

He took my clit in his mouth, his tongue sucking me in, tugging on me while he slipped his finger into me. With his finger slipping in and out, I couldn't believe the feeling. I had never been this open with oral before. In this moment I couldn't open my legs further to him if I tried. I wanted him to touch me everywhere. I could feel my hips undulating of there own will. Telling him what I needed. He gave it. His hands were involved, I don't know how but I know there were many fingers all over me, slipping, sliding me open, exposing me, gliding so easily into me. In this moment the sensations were so intense I didn't care what he did as long as he didn't stop.

My clit has never felt such awareness; I was so in touch with my pussy in that moment. I couldn't believe how intense it hit me. I was cumming before I knew it, there was no denying it, I was moaning, thrashing about while he kept my lower half in his capture. My toes curling, back arching, head back, my mouth parched from panting. His tongue entered me, his fingers playing with my clit, rubbing it mercilessly while he laved up my excitement. Cumming continually beyond my experience, there was no need to even attempt to prolong it, in fact my hips bucked in attempt to cease his incessant sweet torture.

When I calmed down he slid up, his hand cupping me as he came. I could feel the wetness from me all over his hand, its musky scent rolling up with him was turning me on more. As he came down upon me fully laying the length of me, between my weakened and splayed legs, he bent kissing my neck up my jaw and chin to my lips. I could taste myself on him. Drunk on my own taste I wasn't even aware of him raising his hips before he plunged into me.

I screamed out at the intensity, my whole body caught up in the spasms of my inner walls pulsing around him. My body instantly in another orgasm before my mind could catch up. The tremors eventually subsided, the perspiration dried on me before I could move. I lay there useless as an overcooked noodle, not even trying to move into a less vulnerable position.

When I knew I could form a sentence, I asked 'what the hell just happened'

Dave looked at me, smiled and said 'welcome to your Brazilian'

11

Sex with the Ex

Knowing what you're getting

---

ot to beat you over the head with it but I am certain by this point you have gathered; I enjoy sex. I am a passionate woman and it needs an outlet. In my younger years I admit I was freer with my favors. The older I get, the less I want to add to the notches. So, I have found myself on numerous occasions, going back for sex with the exes. It's familiar and irrelevant of who they have slept with it's somehow illogically safer in my mind. I know what I am getting. I know where my heart stands-most of the time.

I will be honest, when I reflect back, some of the best sex I have had (keeping in mind the difference between making love and sex), has been when I went back. Without the bonds of trying to make the relationship work (they are your Ex for a reason), there has been a freedom for me. I guess it boils down to less need for romantic gestures. Often it's accompanied by urgency which supersedes niceties.

Sex on the balcony, sex barely in the front door, sex in a pool, sex in a corridor, jealousy sex – not pretty and very potent, sex in a cabaña, sex in a car, sex when you just plain old know how good it was and can't deny it, cyber sex, phone sex, and booty call sex my mind is flashing to them all.

I have had a creative, and damn good sex life thanks to my ex's, most of which you will meet or have met in a more positive light in other chapters as I tell stories from the list above. For a minute though, let's take this opportunity to shed light on some of the not so fantastic moments. They happened too, and in the case of an ex, it seems way worse than if it happened with your boyfriend. Sex with the ex is supposed to be powerful, liberating, somehow impersonal, unattached after all you are not together anymore so you should be at your best. You're going back for the highlights of your relationship not to add to the lowlights.

My first sex with the ex was the second guy I slept with, probably the least flattering story I could share. He had just broken up with the woman he left me for and he was remembering how fucking fantastic I am. At least that's how I am going to remember it. He called and was going on about stuff and the conversation turned from his relationship to ours. Next thing I know I was running down the stairs and rudely told my friends they had to leave my place. They knew I was on the phone with him and Mac was not impressed that I was shoving them out; she knew I was going to go running and potentially make a fool of myself because I wasn't thinking. I pushed them out anyway, hoped in my car and went to pick him up.

We came back to my place where we began to take off each others clothes with little delay when Mackenzie's words came back to haunt me. In my excitement at the prospect of sex with him I totally forgot I had my period.

Without question this is why he was coming over so my stopping confused him, coupled with my lack of explanation he was likely not impressed. With embarrassment, I finally told him. He didn't seem to care; I on the other hand was grossed out.

After much deliberation on my part I finally acquiesced since I was on my last day anyway. He went to get a towel to make me feel less worried and I changed into a new piece of lingerie I had bought and attempted to erase the last half hour of dampened allure I had created. I was still a little hesitant, not exhibiting the same frantic need from before but was soon enjoying him and was pleased to discover I had nothing to be worried about.

Another more embarrassing story than that one was the first time I ever experienced a queef a.k.a. a pussy fart. One website refers to the noise as cunt trumpet music which I find hilarious even though I will likely never reference it with that terminology verbally. Though I didn't move far off the central topic this time, I will reel you back to where we were before that distracting visual. I am a lover of lubricant, after using some we were going at it when out comes a little pussy fart. There was split second where we both froze and then he continued. I didn't recover quite so quickly. All I could think was holy shit does he think I just farted, is now the time I explain what it was? Does he know? I could feel heat suffusing my face. I now know how natural they are, that I can't control it, if it's anybody's fault- it's his for shoving his dick into me over and over and creating the air pocket. It is something I can laugh at when it happens now or even enjoy, knowing it means we are both fucking like bunnies.

The last story I have on this topic that I am willing to share; my lack of previous control around one ex. It was 2001; we hadn't actually been in a committed relationship before though possessiveness was there just the same from having slept together for most of the year. It was October, I was on a vacation, I had a boyfriend but he wasn't with me. He trusted me to go on this trip alone. All he asked was that I not sleep at my "ex's". I agreed. A group of us went to a party that started during the day and ended up going into the wee hours back at a friends place afterwards. It was there that I blew it. All day I had been near my ex. We gravitated towards each other at this party. I could feel the disapproval from my girlfriend. She was sending warning daggers to me knowing what was happening. I told him I was staying at her place that night; I had made a promise not to stay at his house. He stayed at the party too. We ended up sleeping together in the same bed that night. As difficult as it was to resist the pull between us, nothing happened physically between us other than maybe a little spooning. I felt victorious and proud that I had done the right thing by my boyfriend and had not given into temptation.

That is until the next morning. Yes, me and my morning sex, even disappointed in myself, I couldn't stop the smile, even in the face of my girlfriends chastising look I still couldn't regret it.

Until I got home and couldn't sleep with my boyfriend. We broke up soon after and by New Years I was enjoying my ex again without the guilt.

This is the story of Claire and Brad. Growing up together, they were the best of friends, high school sweethearts. All the storybook perfection, they were the enviable golden couple everyone wanted a relationship like. They got married in their early twenties just after graduating university and lived in matrimonial bliss for a few years.

Then other interests began to pull them apart, and it seemed the only thing that kept them together was the chemistry they couldn't deny. They were the karma sutra personified.

Eventually they realized this was not enough, if they wanted to salvage any part of their relationship they would have to separate. Claire moved out west, pursuing a career opportunity and they were divorced a year later.

Over the next couple years they communicated via emails and phone calls on special occasions. They became friends, each moving on dating new people. Then one Christmas, three years later, Claire was coming home for the holiday and let Brad know.

They agreed to have dinner one night at his place so he could show off his new house.

As luck would have it, there was a crazy snow storm and Claire, not having driven in the snow in the past few years, was weary of driving in it. Brad suggested she stay the night; laughing at her wary look, telling her he had a spare room.

There was definitely a tension between them; this was the first time they had seen each other since the divorce. Though they were no longer in love, there was so much history and the chemistry was still tangible.

Getting past her unease, knowing she did not want to risk going outside or having Brad driving either, she agreed. They stayed up chatting well past midnight. Knowing it was a bad idea, but not wanting the evening to end. Claire sat there imagining him naked and wondering what it would be like to have sex with him just one more time.

When Brad caught her daydreaming he interpreted it that she was tired and suggested they call it a night. Reluctantly, she agreed, after all her thoughts were crazy. Giving her one of his t-shirts to sleep in, she went to the spare room.

She couldn't sleep, knowing he was just down the hall. How long had it been? That man could turn her on like no one else, the mere thought of him, possibly naked and within her reach and she was so wet. She laid there knowing she would not sleep until she did something about it. Question was would she remain alone or go to him. She could just imagine herself sliding onto his hard cock. Her thoughts so frantic and graphic she had to calm herself down. Ok maybe first she would take off the edge herself then go to him.

She licked her lips, her breath already short with anticipation. Sliding her hand down, caressing her breast. She reached over turning on the light wanting to watch herself. She pushed the sheet aside and raised her knees and let them fall slightly apart exposing her dampened center to the air. Starting with a little tease she caressed her calves. She had had a long shower before dinner and had shaved her legs and put on her favorite body lotion. Maybe she had been thinking about this more than she acknowledged before.

Her skin felt so soft and silky, she was so hot and she had not even got to the place that she wanted touched the most, one hand still caressing her breast, her nipples now a dusty rose shade from tanning – how she loved to tan in the nude, leaving her whole body a golden tone.

She ran her hands around the outside of her breasts teasing herself cupping their full weight in her palm. The slight breeze from the open window caused her nipples to pucker. She grazed one nipple, the slight tickle leaving a tingle in its wake. Reaching to the other, the pads of her two fingers rolled over and around until it stood at attention. God she wanted his lips on her. She licked her fingers, touching the tip of her nipple ever so lightly and closed her eyes for a moment allowing her to imagine it was his tongue teasing her.

A shot of excitement went right down her stomach and in-between her legs. Alternately she gently pinched her nipples and cupped herself, her other hand rising from her lower leg up the inside of her thigh. Her touch softening as she got close to the source of her exquisite torture. Her finger tips dipping into her wet heat and trailing lightly up to her clit without touching its most sensitive peak, over and over again, first one finger then two spreading the moisture until she could feel herself swelling in anticipation and then she flattening her three fingers and she swept up from her heat to embrace her clit in one swift sure motion just like his tongue would have.

She could smell her own arousal. She took one of her fingers, covered in her own juices and rubbed it on her nipples, the moisture instantly hardening them to twin points. She massaged them and then reached down again with both hands to pleasure herself.

She could feel her clit and lips all swollen, hot and wet, she rubbed her clit firmly, her stomach muscles clenching with the excitement building, her breath coming short and fast, and her focus solely on the attention she was directing between her legs. Changing the pace and pressure just as it was needed to bring herself to a fast and powerful climax.

Waiting until her breathing returned to normal and her body cooled from its flushed state she began to think about what she was going to do for him now that her edge was temporarily sated.

She could almost taste him in her mind. My god he had a great cock. It was big and full. It took up her whole mouth and that was just half of him. She loved the feel of it in her mouth. It was so silky soft, and in her wet mouth the slide was such a turn on. She loved to lick him, to hear the sounds he made when she was pleasuring him. Using both her hands and her mouth in tandem to stroke him and keep him wet like it would be inside her when she finally took him deep into her body. She must go to him now before she got herself completely worked up again.

His door was slightly ajar so she peeked her head in, he was lying sprawled on the bed the sheets kicked off, he'd turned up the heat for her and it was toasty warm in the house now and about to get hotter still but that's okay they both liked it sweaty. His one hand was tucked under the pillow behind his head the other lay relaxed against his bare stomach. His chest hair sprinkled across his pecks left her aching to run her hands along him and feel the silken hairs slide under her hands. But she gazed on, taking him all in. He was wearing underwear, black, the fitted boxer style that cupped him, even in rest he was impressive and she ached to feel him growing in under her hands. His well muscled legs had always been a turn on for her, feeling their strength through his skin, if she were to just reach out and trail her fingers along their length she knew they would be like rock under a layer of skin, so in contrast to her own softness.

Taking her bottom lip in her teeth she wondered how to start this without awakening him, nervous, not knowing fully if she would be welcome and knowing they both fought so hard the chemistry between them – yet knowing if he didn't say no, how fucking amazing it was going to be.

Best way to go; don't give him a chance to say no.

She climbed onto the bed, he didn't stir. His one leg was tucked under the other knee making a figure four and leaving him open and vulnerable to her touch. She laid her hand on his thigh and held it there for a moment awaiting his reaction. Nothing, so she continued raising it slowly up until she got to the edge of his underwear. He stirred slightly but did not object. Good sign.

Moving further she slid her fingers up and traced around his cock and back down and then up the other side, he shifted again and she could tell that although he was not truly waking – parts of him were responding positively. She trailed her finger up his cock and watched it jerk in answer. Deciding she was ready to be bolder, she cupped him with all her finger tips and then drew her hand up and down slowly. He made a sleepy moaning sound and straightened his bent leg. Just like she wanted him to.

Lifting herself up over him she set her self down straddling his legs. She came in here in just the t-shirt, it came half way down her thighs, she let it pool down around her hips and his leaving her heat open to him. Not lowering herself onto him yet, she bent and began to trail feathery kisses on his chest. She started where his neck met his shoulder. His head turned to the side leaving his neck open to her, she licked him imperceptibly then kissed the same spot, repeating this same action across his collar bone and then down the center of his chest moving south then over to his nipple. She took his nipple into her mouth, while her other hand caressed his chest and played with his other nipple. Sucking him gently, he stirred his hand raising from its resting place on his chest, coming up to cup her head, his fingers sliding into her hair.

Empowered she trailed over to his other nipple repeating a similar tongue circling, teeth nibbling process and then began working her way further south. As she slid lower she allowed her t-shirt covered breast to connect with his body. The soft cotton grazing her hardened nipples eased her need for touch somewhat. She could feel his hardened cock slide up through her cleavage and as she slid further down she eased his underwear down too.

Her mouth quickly found him and her hands gently cupped him, a sharp intake of breath was all the encouragement she needed and she took the tip of his cock in her mouth, loving him, licking him from base to head getting him wet and slippery, sucking on the head loving the feel of him in her mouth, her tongue swirled around him, the smell of him surrounding her.

She loved to just play with him in her mouth like this, running her tongue around him, an unpredictable and flexible appendage to tantalize him. Using both the action of her mouth and her hands to mimic the action her body would make, cupping his balls and gently squeezing them, his hand fisted in her hair the other hand coming down to touch her, to grasp her breast in his hand through his t-shirt.

"Man, I have missed it when you wake me like this" he said

Bending to the side he maneuvered her before she could even protest – not that she would want to – into an inverted position and promptly took her with his mouth, devouring her like she was a long awaited meal. For a moment she reveled in the intense feel of his mouth on her, he tongued all around her, dipping just inside her and then taking her clit and sucking on her. When he inserted his fingers inside, moving them around and stretching her for what was coming, she thought she would cum on the spot. Crying out she dove her head back down and took him in her mouth, sucking him hard, jerking him with her hands, and laving him with her tongue until they were both mindless and slick with the exertion.

Jumping up she pulled him into a sitting position and them promptly impaled herself onto him taking him into her in one swift smooth stroke. Leaving them both gasping and taking a moment to absorb the intoxicating pleasure riveting through her, and then she began to ride him. Not slow, not gradually faster, but hard, take no prisoners, we can do it nice nice later, fuck me now hard.

Taking her lead he grasped her hips in his hands and savagely helped. His hands moving to cup her ass as he shifted their position and threw her down, raising her hips slightly, he was now on his knees pounding into her. She was getting off on the sounds of his thighs slapping onto her widespread thighs. Her own hands went back and forth between clutching at her own breast and grabbing at the bed as she rose up to rotate and meet his thrusts.

Easing back down she lifted her knees higher giving him a deeper access and she reached down between them to firmly ring his cock wither fingers creating more pressure for him and reveling herself in the feeling of the heat and wetness from them. Then he reached down to cradle her ass he lifted her slightly and thrust harder and faster into her. Both of them so hot and sweaty, she ran her hands all over his chest and back loving the feel of the heat generated, knowing they were both so close. Now! she screamed, NOW! He took her mouth in a powerful kisses as he plunged into her taking them both over and emptying himself deep within her.

12

Threesomes

I don't define threesomes traditionally; as three people experiencing intercourse. For me, its just three people enjoying a sexual experience together. More than one person involved at the same time can be mind-blowing. It's easy to get caught up in the thrill and lose track of who is doing what.

The first porno I remember was one with Shannon Tweed, and if you knew how long I spent searching the internet to remember her name you would laugh with me. Even after scrolling her filmography I cannot tell you the name of the film nor the story line either. I have no idea why I even saw the film, how old I was or who I was with, maybe I was seven and was sneaking a peak while my Uncle Ray watched it. No idea, but just like Amityville Horror has stuck with me, so did this one scene.

She was in a room, it was black and next thing I remember she is lying on the floor and all these hands are roaming all over her through black latex, all I remember were these anonymous hands touching her everywhere. I remember being so intrigued by the idea; it definitely shaped some fantasies for me for a long time.

Which leads us to threesomes and the idea of multiple partners all touching. I don't know if I ever told anyone about my fantasy previously but for my first 'threesome' I was eighteen or nineteen, I was in college and I was at a girlfriend's house, her parents were out of town. His name was Steve. I told them while getting drunk, that all I wanted was to be touched from head to toe without getting distracted by my insecurities. A bottle of some random liquor later with another one having been brought upstairs with me, I was drunk. I was also granted that wish.

I have no idea whose hands were where or whose tongue was where and I didn't care. I was in ecstasy. That night was the closest I have gotten to the Shannon Tweed memory.

Probably my most funny multiple partner action; I once had sex beside two friends all on the same bed – that was fucked up. Not because it was all that original, it was just odd. At one point I tied the guys' hands (who I was straddling) together with a belt to stop him from distracting me with what I wanted to do. When that didn't stop him, I then tied him to my girlfriends' wrist with a bandana as she was lying down beside him on the bed. This brought up some interaction between the two of them.

Now although we were all in the same room, and engaging in sexual activities, it wasn't completely interactive between all of us. The guy beside me was Rob. He had not seen me naked before and yet here I was fucking his friend while he fucked mine. I remember looking over at him and both of us were doing the same things to our respective partners. I was still pretty young, it was definitely outside my boundaries leaving me both freaked out and excited and turned on.

When I graduated, we had a chance to put a little blurb in the yearbook along side our photo. I politely thanked the teachers who had impacted me and wrote down the initials of my close friends acknowledging them and then a couple little quotes to remember some events. This one was submitted however it was misread by the yearbook staff. It went in the year book misquoted as, …'Belts and Bananas' not having quite the same tone 'Belts as Bandanas' and yet somehow sending out an entirely other cryptic message. I was truly angry for a bit before I laughed my ass off over it.

A more recent multiple partner action involved a few bottles of wine, pole dancing around a square column, lap dance exchanges for all, some water involving activities, and a big comfy bed. That is the only one where I woke up with both partners; it was odd yet still comfortable. Chalk one up to being turned on by power tools, and rebelling from six months of sex with the lights out.

This story starts off with a few implied possibilities that I wasn't sure if they were suggestions or wishes or maybe both. But when I remember it, the classic porn tune is the soundtrack, bwang chicka bwang waa.

It has the innocent beginning like the pizza delivery boy ringing the bell, but all the players are in place for this story to get dirty fast.

Two totally hot women, and yes one of them is me, the other is the fantastic woman utilizing the band saw as we sit in the garage building some wooden boxes. This lasted a few hours, and then I retired to the house to watch TV while she finished up her project.

Enter in the token 'pizza boy', in this case an Alfa Male, who is up for anything and the couple of beers turn into a bottle of wine and the conversation loosens up, after discussing various altered state experiences and having a group discussion on the merits of color in the room as well as the benefits of turning the room into a kick ass movie room complete with fur throws and lounge beds. Soon after who knows what we were talking about but then we got hungry. Heading downstairs and ordering Chinese we opened another bottle of wine and turned on some Jamie Cullum.

After the third bottle we were discussing my recent exposure with pole dancing and searching out the house for what could be used to demonstrate my now embellished abilities. With new more appropriate music chosen to accompany my embarrassing performance and my thighs still bearing the bruises from the week before learning's, I sauntered up to a square column in the house and proceeded to circle around it feeling pretty damn sexy even though I was not smoothly executing my objective.

With laughter being enjoyed by all, this little session soon inevitably had to stop. That's not to say it doesn't progress. When the column proves to challenging, we moved onto lap dancing to entertain each other and elevate the sexual energy brewing. I have some very amusing photos of our generous gyrations.

At some point I felt that everyone was aware of the possibilities but no one seemed to be making a move to cross a line, so I undid my pants and turned my lap dance into a strip show. Dancing then continued in our undies much to his pleasure, costumes came out and it got turned up a notch, which of course lead to the naked hot tubbing.

Oddly enough this seemed to douse the flames a brewing. None of us are particularly bothered by nakedness and the hot tub was just to damn ordinary for the path we were on. So we got out, she then jumped in the shower and I followed to de-chlorine and have a make out session to get back in the frame of mind we were both going for.

I have no idea what he was doing at this point but after our shower we all ended up in his bed. Arms and legs tangled, everyone making out with each other, who knows whose hands were on whom. I know that night my boobs and hers got some SERIOUS attention. I remember at one point being in the middle and feeling much like a sandwich. He was thrusting against me and she was writhing under me and for a moment I checked out and was like, uhhh, am I just in the way here?

Then I checked back in, rolling around getting out of the sandwich. There was much moaning and groping, but I was also aware that I was the third party. Once in awhile she would leave the room for reasons I don't know and we'd have a make out party of our own, but when it came time for sex, I'm just not that girl who wants to have sex with the same guy the same night so they both left the room and had sex in the living room. I am not sure if this was supposed to be sneaky or what but whatever. We all cuddled up after, laughed at how the evening had transpired and fell asleep together.

For the past couple weeks I have been reading a book whenever I get a moment, called 'I Love You, Nice to Meet You'. I think that sums up that night. In a lot of ways I met two people I already loved that night.

13

Fantasy

Now, means a little longer please.

When I was asked what my ultimate fantasy was all those years ago, my answer was not likely typical. When most people were thinking threesome, or something erotic, a little outside the boundaries of propriety, I was still the shy lover- insecure.

I did not appreciate my body then as I can now. My fantasy then as mentioned, was to be able to be touched from head to toe in pleasure rather than with fear that my body would not measure up. All I wanted was to be loved the way a woman should be loved. Cherished, appreciated, to feel beautiful and wanted.

Now many years later I revisit this same fantasy. This time however, it looks a little different. Yes, I want you to know every inch of my body, I want no spot left untouched, though now I want to be touched in ways I never knew of back then. My passion often finds me to eager to be able to go slow. Creative perhaps, but I've never really role played. In my fantasy, it's slow and a different form of dominance is displayed. Ways only a woman who knows her body can appreciate the anticipation of.

Would you like to know what it looks like?

There will be a large bed, the lighting soft and there will be music, something light maybe a little R&B. I am open to various accessories which would be chosen knowing me as you would.

You would be strong with me though never demanding. Telling me what you wanted me to do, knowing what I want. I would surrender to you; you will have my complete trust. I would do anything you asked. Both of us respecting each others power.

"Remove your clothing for me baby".

With my eyes looking into yours I remove my blouse first. Button by button my skin beneath is revealed. The room is warm though my skin is sensitive to what is happening and goose bumps are breaking out along my arms and I can feel my breasts tighten within my bra, my nipples gathering into tight peaks scraping against their confinement, seeking your touch already. As my eyes close a moment I am thinking about how your lips and tongue will feel on me.

"Open you eyes for me love"

I do, my blouse is open and I remove it allowing it to pool to the floor. My bra revealed, the satin cups pushing my breasts up in offering to you, the mounds desperately seeking attention. Reaching for the zipper of my skirt and sliding it down, the material soon joins the blouse on the floor.

Stepping out from the circle of clothing, they are kicked aside. My g-string panties barely concealing the line of hair leading to the place I most crave your mouth at the moment. I can feel moisture from within escape me, dampening my panties, preparing the way for you to enter me smoothly.

"Would you sit on the bed for me?"

"Yes"

"Sit on your knees sweetheart, with your legs slightly spread and place your hands upon your thighs."

I comply, my heart rate accelerating waiting to see what will be next, wanting so much to be touched and yet seeing the patience in your eyes and knowing it will not happen yet as I want it to.

So used to fast and passionate I am, it is intoxicating for me to find myself so stimulated without yet having had any contact from you and knowing I cannot move this along as I crave. The craving only exciting me that much more and to a place both physically and mentally I have never been.

I can see that you too are turned on; your eyes have darkened with both passion and the control you have been given.

"Would you like to see me as well?" you ask

"Yes"

Giving me the same show I had given you, staring into my eyes as the chest I so love begins to reveal itself. I lick my lips, to give some moisture back to my suddenly dry mouth.

I want so much to touch your skin, knowing its texture, its smell, and taste. My chest rising and falling deeply, and I can see in your eyes you know how much I want you. It's a powerful aphrodisiac.

Unbuttoning your pants; I can see your erection straining for release, quickly filling the opening of your fly as it slides down. Clenching my hands in determination to not reach out and stroke you as I want to. Not to take you into my hands and feel that hard hot and silken length in my palm. Not to remove your underwear myself, you are going so slowly, and I want to take you into my greedy mouth.

Your pants drop and you step out from them.

"Stay as you are" you say, and then you come around the bed, I feel it depress beneath your weight though you remain far enough away that we are not touching. I can feel your breath on the nape of my neck. I can feel the heat from your body along my entire back. What I would give to lean back and let that heat scorch me. My stomach muscles are trembling, my thighs are vibrating, my breath catching while I await your next direction.

"Take off you bra for me sweetheart"

Immediately reaching up behind, anxious to free my breasts from the confining bra, eager for the coolness in the room to offer some relief to my breasts that are aching to be touched. Instead, they feel caressed by the air and harden further almost painfully. I want to give myself the relief you will not.

"Place your hands at the back of your head", it's like you can read my thoughts, further prolonging my want.

I feel vulnerable in this position not knowing what you could be thinking. And then I feel it, a light tickle of material at my hip, teasing me, no pressure, just stimulating. I am going to go mad. I can feel the pressure inside me building; I am close to orgasm already. I know it's a touch away, if you would only stroke, handle, lay your hands on the places that throb for your touch.

Raising the silken material, it caresses my stomach, like a breeze would in summer heat. My breath hitches; I can feel my pulse beating erratically, a flush across my chest, a tingling between my legs that is crying for ease.

The material dances up, between and around my breasts without yet touching the sensitive peaks, wanting to move ever so slightly seeking even the light touch of the silk to caress me.

"No cheating"

"This is torture, please"

With one end of the silk draped across the outer side of my left thigh I can feel you reaching between my legs, the wisp of material skimming along the over sensitized skin at my right inner thigh, trailing from one side to the other and caressing along the string of my panties as you pull it through to my backside. The movement is causing cool air to stir and brush against my wet heat. My thigh muscles go rigid as a whimper escapes me.

My legs actually begin to tremble from the control I am attempting to keep. I can smell the musky scent of my own arousal, biting my lip, my nails digging into my scalp, as you repeat the process again across my other thigh and through my legs again, this time allowing it to graze my swollen center in the process.

And then I feel it, the heat. You are nearer; the mattress dips as you slide up behind me. Your hands reach out finally and you place them just under my breasts, branding me with your touch. An audible intake of breath rushes into my mouth and catches as I indulge by falling into you.

"Sit up sunshine, we are not there yet"

When I do, your teasing hands reward me by inching closer to my yearning nipples. Your hands trail all around and I can feel my breast getting fuller, seeking to fill your hands that are so close to fulfilling my need. Drawing your finger tips to the peaks finally touching me even if ever so slightly. A cry releases from my lips, my back arching, seeking more of your heat and body contact. I can barely see, my eyes glazed over in passion beyond my experience.

"You are mine"

"Yes" it comes out in a strangled whisper

Then you give me a taste of what is truly possible between us. Leaning into me I can feel your incredible hardness at the base of my back and at the same time your hands fully embrace my breasts, enclosing them in the heat of your hands, molding me, lifting my breasts in your palms, massaging them, so many sensations overloading at once, my hands drop, coming around to cup your head, my fingers sliding into your hair feasting on the ability to touch you.

Your one hand slides down my torso and as your mouth touches my neck, your teeth grazing that tender spot at the nape of my neck, my legs already weak, would give way if not for that fact I am sitting already. The moan coming from me, is as natural as my breath. As your hand travels to the edge of my panties and slips underneath, my hips automatically tilt seeking the pleasure from your touch. One finger slides down the line of curls and into the wet path to my center spreading that moisture around. Your hand then escapes leaving me almost crying in want. Until I can hear in your voice how much control you too are exercising.

"Remove your panties for me"

I can feel the strength it must have taken you not to just rip them off but to follow this path we have chosen instead.

Rising up to my knees and then bending over, seeking a little balance to lower the panties down my thighs.

My name escaping your lips on a sharp intake of breath and I realize the view I have unintentionally taunted you with.

Without even fully getting my panties off, you've risen to your knees as well, your hands are on me. One holding me in my bent over position the other using two fingers, rubbing the exposed wetness between my spread legs. I can feel your erection twitch at the intensity of your response to me, tapping the back of my thigh.

With a shift on the mattress, your hands leave me only to be replaced with the solid, hot extent of your erection along the length of my own wetness. As you rub along me at this angle you are sliding right to my clit and the relief is intense, my hips of their own volition ride the length of you without penetrating. Together with my back arching in ecstasy, your hands possessively grasping my hips as your cock thrusts along me, I am in heaven.

Just when I think I may finally get what I want so badly, you pull away and flip me onto the mattress on my back tying my hands to the bed posts with the silk, your head coming down to rain kisses along my stomach. I understand you are desperately seeking to control your desire, to prolong this sweet torture. My legs spread, encasing you; you allow our bodies to remain in contact as we again start the ride.

From my stomach, traveling down over the sensitive hollow at my hips, with light licks your tongue leaves a wet trail, singeing in its path.

Where your hands glide down my legs, your mouth follows placing kisses at my inner thighs. Down, down, raising my leg, you place a kiss at the back of my knee, and with my leg draped over your shoulder, you continue to kiss down to my toes. Stopping there and taking one toe in your mouth, pure bliss. So wet, warm and erotic, I am melting.

Paying equal attention to both sides, you make your way back up my other leg.

It has never been this one sided for me, I ache to touch you, yet I am aroused like never before at being the focus of such detailed attentions and hindered from reciprocating.

Your hair tickles my skin where it precedes your mouth. Hair that is made for a woman to slide her fingers into. If only I could, I would do so and guide you exactly where I want your mouth.

So in tune with me you look up at that moment, your head so close I can feel your breath reacting to the dampness between my legs. Shuddering, my head falls back in delicious torment

You deny me again of my immediate wants, in their place you offer continued caressing, pushing me further than I would think a woman could handle. I feel so on the edge, I am floating, my body tingles all over and feels electric to your touch, not knowing when the next relief will come.

With you in between my spread legs, your left hand comes curling around from under me, over my thigh and hip, down over my stomach, palm open flat against me, two fingers reaching down to stretch my lips open, exposing me. I can't look, I am so desperate for what I want. Without additional warning your flattened tongue takes a long lick up to my clit in one sweep. A scream cried out without me aware it is from my own mouth, my heart momentarily stopped before erratically charging on. Then you take my clit in your mouth. Savoring the bud like it is a butterscotch candy. Suckling it, and alternately flicking it with your tongue, laving up to it. I can feel the juices we are creating dripping down as I scrunch the silk in my hands, unable to thrash as I would if not for the hand at my stomach holding me prisoner to your ever capable ministrations. My heart beating madly I feel it exceeding the confines of my chest, oxygen being deprived from my lungs as I lay gasping for leverage, and then you slide a finger in me. My hips buck strongly against your hold; my head springs forward to watch this incredible happening. Your eyes look up at me and I swear you a smile right before I feel that one finger become two. My head drops back in sheer pleasure as you rotate your fingers inside me touching all the right places, while still stimulating my clit with both your tongue and the fingers holding me open, gently but firmly rubbing around it.

"Cum for me baby, cum for me now"

And as if I had been waiting for permission, I release the grip of my control and give over to you, my stomach convulsing at the intense orgasm that has my insides contracting on your fingers inside me.

Without giving me time to recover as I lay limp, a light sheen of perspiration along my body you run your tongue up my stomach. Licking the underside of my breast, around the outside curve. My body still experiencing aftershock ripples, arches into you, seeking contact. Your hands cup where your mouth has been. So warming, my nipples left untouched reacting to the varied temperature. If I could reach my own breasts at this point I would take them in my own mouth my need is so great. My weakened legs reacting, clenching your hips, even satisfied completely I still crave you inside me fully.

You compromise by moving your body in contact, searing my nipples at the heat of your chest against mine. Renewed energy infuses me as the sweet and seemingly endless perfect agony begins to build up again.

"Please", I ask

"Do you really want it to end baby?"

"I don't know", I can only answer honestly

Raised up over me, and leaning in, you kiss me. Not with the passion I greedily want, but with tenderness we have not shared in sometime. I almost weep at its beauty. It is here, I feel I could stay forever. Your heat against me, your mouth on mine, your tongue loving me. My heads reels and I lose the ability to think completely wrapped in this blinding moment of euphoria.

"You are so beautiful"

Without knowledge of how, I feel my hands free and as I lower them to wrap around you. You slowly enter me at the same moment my arms embrace you. With my one hand in your hair and the other around your shoulders, I am as close to you as I can be. My eyes are closed taking in all the pleasure the moment is.

"Open your eyes baby; look at me while I make love to you"

And like never before I am bonded to you like no other could ever replace. I feel every inch of you slowly sliding in and out of me. As our eyes are locked I no longer know where you end and I begin.

You are in my soul.

14

Getting what you need, however you can

From BOB to beats

I told a man I know about this book and he asked if a particular time we had been together was going to be included. After some consideration I deemed it worthy of the share. I figure enough women out there could identify with 'getting what you need, with or without help'.

This chapter is about looking after your own needs. Sometimes for women that looks like a little Battery Operated Boyfriend (BOB) and sometimes ones own hands and sometimes as in this story below, it was a partner who was sleeping but still functioning.

Before I get there though, Catholicism deems it wrong to pleasure ones self. I know that, not because I am Catholic, but because I heard that once and it has stuck with me since I thought it was so sad. I won't go into the story of how I first learned that rubbing myself felt good, I will acknowledge I was young and thought I would get in trouble if someone found out. But the first time I heard others did it, I was overjoyed, no longer fearing admitting it. Free to explore it, ask questions. Get better at it!

I once had a boyfriend who asked me what I had done with my day. Personally thinking it was HOT, I had shared with him that in-between tasks of laundry and cleaning, I had taken the time to pleasure myself while he was gone.

Appalled, he felt that it was a reflection on my lack of satisfaction with our sex life, like I wasn't satisfied enough with our couplings and therefore had to do it myself. I was astounded to say the least, not feeling that at all, just passing the time really. He said he never did that – my turn to be shocked and thinking – wow you don't know what you are missing.

In my early thirties I finally bought my first vibrator. I was at a sex toy party, not my first, but my first that I bought a BOB. My intentions were of a giving, if ridiculously ignorant nature. I was listening to the woman talk about all the different vibrator options, personally I was looking for remote control vibrating panties for which she didn't have but was happy to order for me until I saw the price, yikes! I'll wait 'till the novelty wears off. Anyway, as she passed around one particular BOB, I heard her say it was waterproof. Instantly my mind went to visions of my more liberated friends who I was going on a trip with. Thinking it a fun party favor I bought it without actually thinking about the logistics.

When I got past the giggle of my fun addition to the party, like a patient coming out of a coma, I began to clue in, eeeew, I cannot share this! Laughing hysterically at myself, I still wasn't going to return it. Girl's gotta have one sometime.

Let me tell you how pleasant that first week was. I put it in my purse and actually forgot about it for a day or two. I was working one day when I remembered it was in my bag and decided to give it its first try on an extended and well needed break. OH Yeah baby, that little wonder made my day a lot more interesting,...a couple times.

I recommend everyone trying one. It's a lovely little addition to the sex life, both alone and with a partner. Ladies, if you are at all shy about masturbating with your partner, this could be your ticket!

Now back to the story

It was somewhere around 8:00 in the morning. The sun was coming in through the picturesque windows and open patio doors that overlooked the ocean. We were on vacation. For all intent purposes it was way too early to get up, I had only had a couple hours sleep. We had partied late the night before, he much later then I had. Waking him up because I was up, seemed down right cruel.

I laid there in the huge king sized bed we were sharing, aware that sleep was not embracing me back into its arms and realized, I was horny. Not uncommon for me, it was after all the morning, but unfortunate timing since he was seriously out cold.

I could hear that beats were still going strong downstairs. There was a group of us who had taken over the estate to celebrate a birthday. Lucky girl, I was sleeping with the birthday man.

Attempting to distract myself I began thinking about how it all came about. We had been friends for a number of years; we had even slept together a couple times the year we met until we each began dating other people. Then he moved away. We kept in touch; he came home to see family a lot. I went on a holiday for my birthday – I like to go away each year for my birthday. Anyways, he came that weekend as well to see the same friends. While there one night he told us about this great party he was planning. I listened excited for him and yet never expecting to be included in it. I was in a reflective place in my life then, quiet, regrouping. When I got the invite to this party I was completely surprised but no way was anything stopping me from going. It was a perfect chance to bust out and get back into life, meet new people and have fun.

There were couples there as well as singles, twenty in total. From the first night, I knew I was going to get laid on this trip, as did most of the others I am sure. I just wasn't sure who with yet. The first night we had stayed in a different hotel as the estate was not ready for us yet. Over the course of that night I had three men in my bed. I say it like that because it's shocking, truth is nothing happened with any of them but it is a hilarious story. Although it's off topic I will share an abbreviated version for amusement alone. I think it also sets the scene for how close friends we all were.

I went to bed earlier than most for two reasons. The first, I was feeling tired, having arrived early with one other friend and we had been in the sun and drinking all afternoon. Two, I was overwhelmed by the energy of the group who had arrived later. They were all so connected and lively, and all but one of them were strangers to me. I wanted to go to sleep so I would be in a better energy and on the same page the next day.

We had a few suites for the group, no one was really assigned anywhere. There was only one queen bed in each suite and sofas and twins also available. I had decided to sleep in the queen bed in the suite we choose when we arrived first.

My room had a window that opened to the courtyard, I lay there listening to the party going on outside as I began to drift off. I was awoken by a little knock at the door and a voice, 'hey are you asleep' to which I replied 'no' and then the voice asked if they could come in. I said yes and rolled over and went back to sleep not even caring who it was just figuring I knew them and they wanted a place to crash. He crawled in and snuggled up to me. It was the birthday man.

What felt like minutes later and could have been hours I was awoken by a little knock at the door and a voice, 'hey are you asleep' to which I replied 'no' and then the voice asked if they could come in, I said yes. It struck me as somehow odd and yet before I could place the déjà vu a voice from immediately behind me said 'hey' and then I realized it was not déjà vu but two men who were now there. The birthday man and the friend I had first arrived with, who I had been flirting with that day. He crawled in too. We all went to sleep or had tried to when I heard a knock on the door. Laughing, I rolled over and a third guy, a friend of all of ours said 'hey, whatcha guys doin?', we all rolled onto our sides he came in and we played word games, eventually I think we all slept some. Around six a.m. the last guy to have arrived left, then the second to arrive left and eventually the first. I was alone in the bed again laughing, and knowing I was still not going to be at my most refreshed that day but at least I would be laughing.

We moved over to the estate around noon, I brought my bags to one of the villas. After I was somewhat unpacked and feeling sorted the birthday man had come up to me, kissed me and asked if I wanted to stay with him that night. And so started my sexual escapades with him again.

The first night left me pretty tender but after a day of rest we were at it like bunnies, in the shower, in the bed, I am even on film going down on him in the pool. No wonder I couldn't get sex off the brain for long.

I laid there thinking about all of it that horny morning. The beat continued drifting up through the open door of our villa. Seemed some people were either on a fifth wind and still going, or had slept and were up and going again. It was a crazy fantastic week. A week of complete liberty and escapades I had never before explored. Had you told me a week previous that this is what I would have done, I would not have believed you.

Yet there I was, feeling powerful and wanting the next adventure.

I laid there naked and even hornier than before. The beat reached in my soul, pumping my blood into a new rhythm, and not being denied. I was full of energy, I wanted to dance, I wanted to run naked around the pool, I wanted to have fantastic sex and I wanted some of the fresh fruit I knew would be waiting for us at breakfast. This got me back to thinking about sex, sex and fruit, licking the juices off each other as we shared it. I could no longer deny the need for sex right then and with the fantastic man right here beside me so peaceful and unaware of my intentions.

I reached down between my own legs and sure enough I was as wet as I felt like I was. Beyond ready, I ground myself into my own hand seeking to ease some of the excitement. I turned to him, he was still out cold. I trailed my hand down his torso, not a single twitch. I reached down to take him in my hand. He was soft and yet I knew I could change that. Looking up at him once more I began to play with him, caressing him, gliding my hand and trailing my fingers along him as he slowly responded, growing longer and firmer in my hand. I continued to watch his face to see if he was rousing. Unbelievable he was not though his body was and I decided as selfish as it was, in that moment this would work for both of us, he could sleep and I could get what I needed.

I pleasured him until he was hard with both my hands and my mouth while he incredibly appeared to remain out cold. I then crawled on top of him, my back to him, facing the stunning view and slid onto that hard cock.

It was unbelievably pleasurable. The beauty before me, the beat pumping through me, the man deep and thick inside me.

I began to ride him in tune to the beats coming in my window. Eventually I even lost awareness of him, I stopped waiting for the moment he became aware and just pleasured myself on him. I loved that he was so cooperative with my needs.

I think I fucked with less inhibitions then I ever had. That music got into me and I just danced on his cock. My hands up in the air, dancing away, I just didn't care

With my feet planted on either side of his legs and me squatted above him I danced, I gyrated, I ground into him, I thrust, and I rode him like I couldn't get enough.

It was a naked dance party and I was rocking it!

There is something about having sex to music. Not like when guys get all smooth and put on the Barry White and set a sexy mood, but taking that dance beat into your soul and expressing yourself through it, HOT!

I was having a great time, my legs burning with the exertion, my body all sweaty from the workout I was enjoying, and then I felt or heard him wake up.

At the time my back was still to him, he'd opened his eyes to the vision of me riding him, my arms still raised and hands thrust in my hair in sheer rapture, my hips thrusting, with a sheen of perspiration all along my back having obviously been at this awhile.

I am not sure exactly what went through his head as he realized I was completely and without shame using his body while he slept, but after acknowledging he was awake he just let me continue. Though he didn't actively participate, or join me in my dance he was getting something out of this as well. I could hear his pleasured grunts, felt him tilting his hips at times, not having the energy to give more, his hands coming to rest at my hips. He let me keep the control; enjoy my ride until I was spent.

When I brought myself to orgasm I flung myself down onto him and then slowly dragged myself off him and back onto my side of the bed. My legs shaking with the after effects of my efforts, and as I lay there catching my breath and reveling in my own talents he laughed and asked if I had enjoyed using him. I smiled, said yes and we both went back to sleep for a couple hours.

Don't feel bad for him; he got plenty of sex that week that he initiated. I think he was too amused to be upset that I had used him.

15

Internet Relationship

Internet chemistry versus physical history

If you've ever gone on a blind date you will know this feeling. That moment when you see the person you are supposed to be hooking up with. It goes one of two ways; incredibly excited licking your lips, I just won the lottery feeling or oh shit how long will I have to invest in this evening before I can deek out.

The same can be said for internet dating. You have been chatting back and forth for months and then you decide to meet. Even though you know he says all the right things, will Romeo be the man of your bedroom fantasies? Will there be physical chemistry to match the mental? Will he look anything like you made him out to be, will he actually look like the photo he sent you? I hate it when people photograph better then they look in person. It's so deceitful.

Now this story is not a fair one. I admit that, it is however the story of a relationship that developed on the internet.

We made arrangements to spend a weekend together. I was looking forward to it. Truly, excited and down right giddy.

Life intervened, and my choices from there created an interesting disregard for innocence, there is a sub-story that explains everything. If I leave it solely about him and don't tell the sub-story, well it's less dramatic, and would be harder to understand why it turned out as it did. I will tell the sub-story afterwards.

So there I was waiting for my internet man. My situation was a step easier in one way, and harder in another. I had met Joel already once before. I knew what he looked like, knew that I was attracted to him. When I originally met Joel, I was on vacation and I had just gotten out of a relationship about two weeks prior with a guy that was so opposite from me it's kind of funny. I was on a trip that my ex and I were supposed to be on together. I had already had my post relationship fling the night before. So, on that next day when I met Joel, I knew I was not going to hook up with anyone that night. I was not looking for another vacation fling to notch on the proverbial bedpost. I am just not that type of girl. So at the party, I did everything I could to not be interested. Only, I was. And based on his attentiveness, so was he.

I stayed true to myself and my vow to not get involved and waited at least a couple days and until I was home out of temptations reach before I contacted him via email and our relationship began. Based on results, I have a thing for being interested in men who live in a city that's not mine. I live in Vancouver and in the past five years I have been interested in a man in Alaska, Phoenix, London, Victoria, Seattle and California. Joel was no different in this regard, we had met when we were both away on vacation, and he lived three thousand miles away from me. We had a phone and email relationship for six months.

Then Joel decided to change careers, and was offered a job that would transfer him a lot closer to me. Not to say that was the reason he took it by any means, it just worked out well. I was finally about to see him again. We were meeting again in the city we had originally met, where we both had mutual friends. Now that I was open to the chemistry flying, what was it going to be like...? There was pressure.

Knowing we would finally see one another my brain had been creating very entertaining images for my pleasure in the weeks leading up. The long distance from Joel had worked out great, after my little fling, I wasn't ready to jump into a physical relationship and because I didn't think we would see each other anytime soon I could say whatever I wanted to him over the internet. It was safe to explore and be vulnerable and a little naughty at times. Now six months later I thought I was ready for these written and imagined fantasies to become reality. But it was a dichotomy, he knew so many things about me, I was totally attracted to him and yet we had never even kissed.

How does one greet a man who already knew so much about you? A man that I knew I wanted to find out what was between us in the hot and heavy sector. Do I just pounce? Would he? As you can tell, I was the talkative one in the relationship and though I knew it had progressed for him as well, who knew if he was sharing the same quandaries.

God, it had been awhile since my heart fluttered and I was nervous. I thought to myself that it would not be an attractive re-first impression, me sweating like a hockey player in an overtime game. I needed to get control of myself.

I tried to distract myself from the eager sweat glands and focus instead on my depleting pre-meeting drink and the merits of whether to have another or not, before I left to meet him. I of course had been ready early as was my unfailing habit. That of course led to the option of two drinks before having to go meet him. Being drunk could indeed make the first moment go a lot smoother. I would be much better behaved if I was not thinking, or shall I say not over analyzing each moment.

I walked in the door of my friend's home. This is where we had arranged to meet up. There he was, standing not ten feet from me. In that moment I knew. It was not going to be as I thought; the chemistry I had so hoped for was not reaching out and pulling me over.

I tried to dismiss it; the cab had taken forever, making me late. I am never late and I was in turn frustrated and out of sorts. Maybe that's all it was. I hugged both friends whose home I was at and then proceeded over to him. It all felt like slow motion. It truly could not have taken me the length of time it felt like for me to go to him. Did he notice? What was he feeling? I hugged him. He hugged me back, kiss on the cheek too.

Now what? The dreaded how do I get through this evening was upon me. On top of that I had committed to staying with him for the weekend. How did I do that to myself? I told myself to relax, I was overreacting. It would all be great. I was practically in love with this guy on email.

We went to dinner, chatted easily. I learned stories through our friend, of their childhood together. Before I was ready, it was time to go back to the Hotel.

Again the panic had returned. What now? Looking at him, it looked as if everything was fine. I could not believe how uncomfortable I was with the concept of talking to him about what was going on for me. This was a man I had been having very intimate conversations with for months. I had sex with him in my mind numerous times. Reality was different though.

We got to the room and I put my little overnight bag down. Luckily it was late by this time. I changed into a tank top and left my panties on and crawled into the bed. He got into bed as well and we ended up making out a bit. I hadn't kissed a new guy in a long time. I enjoyed those "first unknown' moments, when you have no idea how the other person kisses and are pleased to find out that he doesn't kiss like a fish. It was nice. It didn't rock my world enough to compel me to throw my hesitation aside. After a bit, I pulled back, he let me; we chatted a little and went to sleep.

We got up in the morning and went back to my girlfriend's place to get ready for the day. We didn't get ready at the hotel because we were going to a festival where everyone would be in costume and it's more fun to get ready with a few people when costumes are involved. I believe that he enjoyed himself watching us putting different outfits together. When we were suitably attired, we left and met up with friends already there.

The weather was outstanding and we had a good day, dancing, enjoying the sunshine outside and listening to the various artists. Through out the day we bumped into many friends that were there as well. By six, I was ready to go get some real food and it was winding down anyways. Five of us went and grabbed dinner at one of my favorite Mexican restaurants.

I knew that later that evening the festivities were continuing at various venues and many were going to meet up again in a few hours to go to a club, but after a day full of dancing, and sunshine I had no energy left to go into the wee hours as I knew they would. We had also not really spent much time alone and I wanted to, so we went back to the hotel.

I had my computer with me so we agreed to watch a movie that I had brought for the flight: 'The Notebook', girlie I know. Before that I wanted to freshen up, get rid of the sunscreen and grim from a day of dancing. I took a quick shower. I was in the washroom washing my face when he walked in naked. Yes, I said naked. To say I was stunned or shocked would be an understatement. I am not sure I contained my surprise well, but he didn't seem bothered. He was completely comfortable. I wasn't sure what to do with that.

Having been together non stop for twenty-four hours I was feeling more at ease and hanging out with him was comfortable, but I still wasn't ready to have sex, or hang out naked with him. So, I ignored that he was and we watched the movie in bed. When it was over we got into a little heavy petting, some clothing was removed and yet I was just not feeling what I felt like I should be. I was not there, I was not giving this guy the credit or attention he deserved and I was certain I was not going to sleep with him out of some unfounded guilt.

The guy was HOT, had the abs of Adonis, he was funny and charming and he obviously wasn't the one having issues. This is where the male versus female thing comes in. In general; women need to feel some kind of connection, men need to have a hard on. I know that's a blanket statement and half of you reading this may not agree. I don't agree with that statement all the time either but in this case, it is how I felt. I really did want it to work, I thought of the feelings I had for him in the past six months, I thought of all the things I had written and said to him. I brought to mind how I felt imagining all the scenarios that I had created in my mind. I couldn't make it transfer; maybe I just couldn't relax into it. Bottom line, the chemistry just wasn't there for me. Believe it or not, I stopped things again and we went to sleep.

When I woke up in the morning, I knew as much as I enjoyed morning sex, I wasn't going to go there. It was eight when I woke up, I had to leave by ten thirty. I woke him up around nine by giving him a hand job, we made out again for awhile. It was a nice morning even if it wasn't the sex we both were likely thinking about. I told him I had to go. It was nine thirty. I got dressed; he threw on some clothes and walked me down to a cab. I kissed him goodbye and left.

I left him a message a couple weeks later, we maybe exchanged an email or two after that and then he wished me well and that was it.

Now for the sub-story...

A couple weeks prior to that trip I received a phone call; a friend was in turmoil dealing with a personal problem. I listened and said what I could and told him I was there for him. He lived where I was going on vacation; we made plans for him to pick me up at the airport.

I should mention now he was also my ex from two years prior. We had both been in other relationships since. And yet we did what came naturally, we had sex. It was incredible. He was in such an emotional place it was just very giving and intense. We spent the day together and then I left.

A few of us ended up at the same concert the next night, it was there that he found out my plans with Joel for the weekend. I could see the moment when it sunk in, I was potentially going to sleep with another guy all weekend. It wasn't that he wanted me back, it was just he didn't want anyone else to be with me. And, I was going to do it on his turf.

I felt for him and where he was at emotionally- but we had moved on and Joel was important to me too.

When I saw Joel, and did not feel the chemistry immediately, I thought of my ex, that sleeping with him had thrown me off. I felt like I could shake it off, I just needed to be with Joel and reconnect to our own energy.

The next day when we went to the festival, my ex was there. We didn't spend the day together but bumped into him and other friends occasionally throughout the day. I introduced them at one point. That was incredibly awkward. Joel was so great and open, he knew it was my ex. They shook hands and then shortly after, my ex left. I was on pins and needles, guilt mixed with pain for what I knew my ex was feeling and guilt for the knowledge that I had slept with him and Joel had no idea what he was up against.

When I left, my ex texted me, 'That was hard. Be happy' I should have felt better, he was letting me go, I could let go of the guilt. We had dinner, and went back to the Hotel. I just couldn't shake thoughts of my ex, what was he doing, was he ok? I had totally allowed him to fuck with my head. His emotion was real, I am not saying it was intentionally manipulating but it produced the same result.

The part I forgot to mention yet, I had extended my trip to include a week in Wine Country, and my ex was driving me the next morning. I knew I was going to see him and have all these answers soon and yet I couldn't shake it.

When I left the next morning, I took a cab to my ex's place; I used my key and crawled into his bed where he was still sleeping and curled up to him. We spent the next week talking about our emotions around each other. How we both kept a hold on each other that wasn't fair if we weren't going to move forward together.

I called Joel after I had come to grips with my feelings for my ex. I told him in an email that there was another man in the picture. I didn't tell him who, there was no point. He was understanding, told me he had been dating others as well, it was cool. I felt like an ass but held onto the out he was offering me. He wished me well and that was it.

16

Cars

Cramped, creative and urgent

I don't know about you but the first time I had sex in a car I felt surprisingly original. Knowing it has been done since the invention of cars didn't dissuade me from feeling I was doing something no one else had thought of or gotten away with.

Weather it was in some abandon parking lot, an underground garage, the side of a road, I think my most unique was at a garbage dump in the back of a van. My most visible was the time on a major road. Okay it was two in the morning though people I am sure saw parts of me I cannot see without a mirror. After all, front seats don't have a lot of maneuver room and sometimes your tail is up in the air.

I remember my first real good venture into the car territory. I was fifteen I think and he was seventeen, I had just left a family diner and we were in a parking lot by our high school. We started off talking and then making out and then trying to find a foothold for the fully clothed dry hump session.

I have most definitely gone through various stages of being anal retentive in my life. I laugh now when I think of the time I planned to have car sex to the point I brought a dampened napkin in a zip lock baggie to clean up after and to throw out the condom in. I distinctly remember the look on his face when he realized what I had in my hand, that "oh my god who the fuck is my girlfriend" and then the "kick ass, my car is getting christened" look that replaced it.

As I have gotten older the car sex option is no longer the thrill of getting caught, it's simply a matter of I cannot wait to get where we are going to have you inside me and it has to happen NOW. It's an entirely different high and one that leaves me hot just thinking about it.

A few shots of tequila, one I believe was taken from a girlfriend's cleavage and I was feeling no pain. I had come away on vacation only to befriend a woman in the bar who was from my hometown. I am full of moments like this. After having a few animated conversations on a variety of subjects and filling up on my quota of mixed alcoholic concoctions it was tingle time. That time of night where I feel invincible, I feel sexy and plainly put: have sex on the brain. Looking around I saw all the people I would normally flirt with. You see I don't need to have sex at this point, though there is a desire to expel sexual energy. That can look like talking to other hot friends about sex, reminisce about great romps, or just plain old go flirt with someone.

This night I honestly don't remember what my plan was, though I ended up getting into a serious conversation instead. As I leaned in further to hear all the details in this loud bar I was both excited and happy about the tale that was being shared to me.

And then it happened. I looked up; I looked into the eyes of a man I had the most incredible energy with. For a moment I swear time stood still, we were the only ones there, it was like the world just shut off and I could do anything and no one would notice. Our own private bubble.

Unfortunately that is not true, everyone could see everything and I sat there making out with a man I should not be making out with at that time, all I could think was fuck this man kisses exactly like I do. Like he is making love to my mouth.

He tasted of beer and the unique taste that is his and I most likely of the tequila shot I had been sipping and trying to get down for the past 20 minutes but I think I could have easily continued to kiss him forever. His tongue was warm and wet and slid over mine like you would lick your favorite ice cream. When we parted, I licked my lips and just thought this man is fucking yummy AND, I gotta take a minute here.

In the loo I was thinking ok, I know I want this man and should not go there, and at the same time I also knew I had been thinking about this mans cock in my mouth for months. I gave myself an extra little pressure with the tissue paper and washed my hands, expelled a breath of energy and left to go join the festivities again and maybe take my mind off my wayward thoughts, as they could only lead to trouble.

Returning to the bar, I found out it was closing time and the group was moving onto another party. Everyone making arrangements and exchanging address info, I found myself outside and coincidently getting a ride with Mr. Forbidden.

Ok, no problem, its just a ride to a party, nothing is going to happen. I can control myself and do the right thing.

Yeah, ok. Within five seconds you'd think we had been long lost lovers parted at war, we were all over each other. What follows is a scene that could easily make penthouse when described in its graphic details.

Forgetting that we were on a major street and people who were leaving the bar were walking past us to their own vehicles, we made out like addicts and then proceeded to grant each other some fairly intense oral satisfaction.

I know there are times when women give a blowjob because it will get them something, but honestly, I don't. I will only give one when I really, really want to. Otherwise I won't do a good job. In this moment, his cock was like my favorite dessert and I just wanted to savor it. I wanted to feel it both in my hand sliding the skin over the rock hardness of him, and then I wanted to feel the texture of it slide against my tongue. I wanted to taste that slight saltiness, swirling my tongue over his tip, licking him all over and then plunging it into my mouth as much as I could take. Closing my eyes I reveled in finally having this again. It had been almost a year since I had given a blowjob, and I especially enjoyed giving one to him.

It was all very fast I am sure even if it felt like we sat there offering public shows for much longer, after an equally rewarding sugarpuss session we decided to stop and go to the party.

That lasted all of two minutes before I decided I was not done and wanted to enjoy the "offer head while driving" experience. Having no idea where we were headed, I didn't know how much time I had available to do this, I still thoroughly enjoyed it. If the moans were my only indication, I would have known he was having a hard time driving under my ministrations. When we abruptly pulled over and quickly both came to be in the passenger seat with my skirt up around my waist and his cock deep inside me, I knew just how much I had affected him.

There is something to be said about sex in a car. It's awkward to find placement for limbs and it's far from comfortable. But if you are as passionate as we were in that moment – you just plain old don't notice any of it. You just fuck like mad because its going to take to long to get anywhere else that you could do justice to what is going on inside you in that moment.

There is an intense need that drives me, a passion that urges me on to do things I normally might not do. The added thrill of being in public - I swear if we were not in an abandoned lot, my screams could have been heard all over the neighborhood. Fuck that man was just yummy.

17

Cyber Sex

When a little cyber flirting sparks fire

What did we do before the internet? Ok we have heard all the stories about when our grandparents walked through five feet of snow and two miles to the nearest neighbor to even see if they wanted play when they were younger- then came the telephone.

With the telephone you had to wait until you got where you were going or for them to come home or get to work to be able to ask a friend what they were doing later, until the cell phone came.

Even with the cell phone, it was pretty hard to have phone sex during the day for fear your co-workers would overhear you.

Then came the internet and with it instant messaging. You could do it and look like you were working. You could type dirty messages and no one was any the wiser as you sat there perhaps slightly flushed but with a look of innocence plastered on your face.

The world of cyber sex is upon us, and in this day of safe sex practice you can get your rocks off without fear of pregnancy or disease as you hook up with your favorite handle online.

Ok, so that's taking it a bit far. However, in the beginning stages of love or lust, when you cannot stop thinking about each other naked, messenger provides an interesting diversion in an otherwise monotonous day until you can once again be united and fuck like the rabbits you have become.

I speak of this in the third person, but I am far from a cyber virgin. I have passed many an hour away telling my guy de jour just how I want him to stick it to me. From flowery to raunchy, it's been done. And bless the little emoticons that add graphics to the dialogue.

It helps when you have friends who although they are important in their companies, still find the time to search out the latest depictions of sexual y explicit emoticons and pass them onto me. No matter how long I have searched, I have yet to tap into the free world of porno emoticons on my own. Thanks to them, I do have a cute collection. I have refrained from adding the Purple Dinosaur does Debbie to my collection but I have a variety of ass slapping, boob flashing, knob gobbling, pussy licking, doggie stylin, and ride em cowboys to get me through a decent session of cyber sex on messenger and a good enough imagination has gotten me through email sex.

At 3:20 in the afternoon dirty little exchanges in an MSN conversation got her mind spinning longer tales that they didn't have time for in an Instant Message conversation. After some naughty emoticons depicted some fun they could have, the conversation somehow ended in a question that even though he didn't have time, she had the mind to answer. She proceeded to write him an email of exactly what was firing through her brain. All inspired by the leading question;

...what would you like my tongue to do?...

Definitely a question worth answering. She knew she had all the thoughts right there in her head, if only she could say them out loud. Tell him all the things she could see. It came in flashes. His mouth, so soft yet able to give her so much pleasure. She loved kissing, it was so erotic. Whether it was slow and sliding or hard and passionate she just loved to kiss. And kissing him was fantastic. Sometimes you find a man who doesn't necessarily kiss just like you, but fits the way you kiss really well. This was him. He gave when she wanted, and took when she wanted. He'd let her play and then flip her where he wanted to be. Mmm she could close her eyes and imagine. Playing over memories she had already enjoyed with him and interlacing it with things she knew they would both like and hadn't necessarily done yet. Hmm a little fantasy to entertain herself while she passed her day at work, until she could see him again...

Entering the front door of his place, the lights were dim and a lone candle was lit on the table in front of where she saw him sitting on the sofa, she smiled, said hello. She removed her jacket, hung it up, took off her shoes and walked over to him. He didn't get up; she had a look that said she liked him where he was. She stood in front of him, letting him know she didn't plan to sit down and watch TV. Then without preamble she sat down on his lap, her skirt rising as she spread her legs on either side of his. Taking his face in her hands she bent forward and took his mouth. Slanting her head to the right and his to her left, she deepened the kiss. Pulling back for just a second, enough time to look at him and let him see her lick her lips she then lowered her head and licked his. His mouth opened for her as she wanted, and she slipped inside his mouth, his tongue met hers half way. Locked in a slow, tasting glide of tongue on tongue she felt her heart rate quicken, her pulse racing. With one hand reaching back to cup his head, she pushed herself down into his lap. He responded by sliding his hands up either side of her thighs, slipping them up under the hem of her skirt.

Her mind racing with thoughts, getting ahead of herself, imagining all the places he could be touching her, all the pleasure he loved to give. She clenched her legs in response and ground her heat into him again needing the pressure to relieve the tension building within. She could feel him hard beneath her and her body craved him inside her but she knew both of them would revel in the process a little longer before both receiving all they wanted. Getting distracted from the bliss of his kisses as his hand crept further she waited for him to notice her surprise. When his hands reached up to grasp her hips she felt the anticipated pause, sliding to cup her ass he knew then she had not worn panties knowing how much it would turn him on. With his hard cock jerking against her, she knew she had anticipated correctly. Sliding his hands along her ass and then grabbing her hips in his hands he pressed her down into his hardness as he thrust up to meet her. His nostrils flared and she could tell he was taking in the scent of her. Her head falling back, she moaned when his need to taste her took force and he trailed his tongue along her exposed neck while kissing her.

The moment switched from slow and sensual, becoming mad and urgent. Wanting to feel him, his skin against hers she fumbled to unbutton his shirt, did the man ever wear pullovers? As she worked on his buttons while still kissing him she could feel him raising her shirt hem up as well. Frustrated and wanting it now she took a second to pull her shirt off for him and as she went back to his buttons he reached up to cup her breast in his hand. She instantly stopped and savored the feeling evoked by the contact of both his hand on her bare skin and the sensation of that skin being her breast, it sent tingles directly from her nipple to her throbbing clit. He cupped both her breasts given that he had the space to do so, her hands had become limp on his shirt front, buttons forgotten while he shaped and kneaded her breasts. Her back arched of its own volition as he lowered his head to take first one and then the other nipple into his mouth, suckling her, tasting her, rolling the hardened nub around his tongue. Ah yes his tongue, he didn't need direction, he knew exactly what to do with his tongue. Had he not proven that time and time again. She felt like he knew her better then she did at times he could anticipate her needs before she could put voice to it. My God he had a magical tongue. She smiled to herself, her brain once again able to focus on more then just her breast.

Back to his buttons, finally she'd freed the last one and she pressed into his chest, luxuriating in the feel of his chest against her own. She allowed herself to slide up along him, the hairs on his chest providing the sweetest soft friction against her tightened nipples while it tickled alongside her sensitive breast stirring awareness straight down to the heated juncture between her legs.

It was then he decided to take over and shifted their positions, flipping her down onto her back – she loved it when he took charge, he moved her to the top end of the sofa, slid down and spread her legs to accommodate the width of his shoulders. He glanced up at her; with a devilish grin on his face he then bent his head down and began to deliver the sweet torture of his immensely capable tongue. She writhed beneath his ministrations and he had to wrap his arms under her legs and up around her hips to hold her right where he wanted her and keep her from squirming as he nipped and licked and rubbed her in all the right places. He used his fingers to open her lips further to him and circled her clitoris with his tongue, taking the little bud into his mouth and suckling it, tonguing her and rubbing her clit again and again. She knew he was in the mood to take her over the top more then once when she was at the brink of her first orgasm he slid a finger inside her; the combination of the two drove her over the edge instantly. Screaming his name he continued to not allow her to catch her breath as he then slid a second finger in creating some magical movement that had left her physically incapable to handle the intense euphoria she'd found herself at. His fingers mocked the action that was yet to come, her head thrashed from side to side as her second orgasm hit in quick succession.

Unable to speak she attempted to get him to stop fruitlessly she waved him to move up her body. Eventually she got his attention; she pulled on his arm and guided him to where she wanted him. Only then did she see that he still had his pants on. As she kissed him, tasting herself on his lips she reached down and removed his pants and took hold of him in her hand, she wanted to feel his cock take the place his fingers had effectively been. He grasped her hand to stop her, and she whimpered her frustration. You'll get what you want soon enough, I'm not done playing yet he said. Woman would kill to be in her position and she was complaining? Her body hummed, she allowed him to set the pace but wrapped her legs around him to effectively press him to her to, he obliged for a second and rubbed his hard cock along her wet center to alleviate some of her need before he pulled back and put space between them again. His hands came up to caress her breast, teasing her by not paying any attention to the sensitive tips instead he left them tingling, begging for his touch. He kissed her firmly and with promise, fully in control of her still. He raised her hands up over her head, momentarily pinning them in place to let her know to keep them there and slid his hands down her arms. His lips left hers and trailed downward. Her chest rose up hoping to guide him, let him know what she wanted, he indulged her and took her breast into his mouth, swirled his talented tongue around the aching tip. She sighed in relief, her hand without thought came down to cup his head to her, the other unconsciously cupped her other breast in offering to him. Again he gave her what she wanted. Almost delirious with satisfaction she barely saw the glint in his eye before he pushed off the sofa drawing her up onto her weakened legs.

With them both standing, he turned her around and guided her to lean against the dinning table bending her over he hiked up her rumpled skirt exposing her nakedness without removing it. The tips of her breasts grazed the wooden surface which was cold and smooth yet provided an odd and tantalizing friction. Her arms bent at the elbow and she balanced her weight on the table top. She turned her head looking over her shoulder at him in anticipation of the direction this would go.

He smiled, rubbed a small circle on her ass and then gave her a little spanking. She jumped a little, the contact stimulated her and brought her back to a playful energy, and she too smiled and turned her head back to face forward. She knew he would finally fuck her from this position so she was prepared for his finger as it slid along her lips. Opening her up, he spread the wetness and heat he'd created, she was so hot for him she wriggled in her eagerness.

Her back arched, hips tilted and legs spread further apart, she braced herself for the slow slide of him into her. She moaned aloud at the incredible pleasure it gave her, she almost came to orgasm again from penetration alone. Both of them held the position a moment and enjoyed the glove like fit while they gathered their ability to hold on for more. Her legs were barely able to hold her upright, he grasped her hips to support her and held on while he slowly withdrew and then plundered back in. She cried out in rapture at the pleasure he evoked within her.

Done with him having all the control she lifted herself from the table top where she'd been draped onto, braced her arms, and began to rock into him using the table's edge for leverage. Back and forth she took him deeper, he moved up closer to her and braced his own hands on either side of her, housing her in the circle of his arms as she tossed her head back and blissfully continued to gyrate her hips having him touch every cell in her heated center. Raising one hand to her breast he pulled her back against his body and moved them over to the wall where he spread her legs once again and placed her hands on the wall above her while he fucked her mindless. The pace increased and she knew before he told her, that he was going to cum so she let herself go over the edge when he did. Feeling she could no longer stand on her own so overwhelmed by the shattering orgasm that had taken her, she was grateful when he somehow found the strength to take them both to the sofa where they collapsed in an exhausted heap.

Yes, that would be a great night she thought, he is going to love this email. =)

18

Voyeurism & Exhibitionism

Creepy or normal?

There are various levels of voyeurism and exhibitionism. Many of which are harmless and we have all done them. Think about it a second, how many times have you watched a couple making out in public, or been that couple. For the voyeur, it may be a passing glance or a moment when you think you wish you were doing that. You may get turned on subconsciously by it enough to go home feeling randy and jump on your partner.

Are you even aware you are doing it right now? This book is filled with stories that you would likely never sit and watch if it were happening in front of you but handed to you like a dirty magazine and you are curled up in the chair wondering what is going to be said, what dirty little secret will be revealed and in what detail.

By nature we are all curious, it's how we learn. The key is to be open about it, and then it becomes acceptable. It's the people who sneak peeks that give the voyeur a bad name and the exhibitionist no power.

When I was four years old, it was still the seventies; my parents would take me and my eight year old sister to a nudist resort to go camping each summer. I grew up around naked people. I didn't understand it to be not the norm until I was older. For a number of years I reverted like a turtle into my shell and was embarrassed to be caught not fully clothed. My first exposure to nudes was certainly not Pamela's gravity defying breasts, no, I knew naked to be all shapes sizes and colors. Even knowing this, I was still shy.

When I was thirteen my mother had remarried and now went to a different resort, I was going no where near there. First off I was in puberty and the idea that I would willingly parade around my budding breasts and random pubic hairs was ludicrous. But I remember going up with her one day because we had to be there to meet the phone guy. I had brought along a girlfriend for moral support. I refused to be outside where naked people were so we sat inside and as I looked out the window I saw a rather round man doing his daily walking exercises. As he walked he would reach into the air with one hand and then the other. He was wearing a t-shirt; I thought I was safe until I glanced down further and noticed with a gasp that he had no shorts on. As his hands rose, his flaccid penis would come into view like a peek-a-boo game. I swiveled around in guilty embarrassment I am not sure who more for, him or myself. My girlfriend just laughed and shoved me out of the way to look herself.

When I was about eight, I would sneak out of bed to see what my babysitter was watching. Bedtime was always prefaced with 'time for bed, its adult TV time'. This is how I first saw Porky's.

I guess the next stage of V&E would be threesomes - may seem like quite the jump but not really. You're involved so there is entitlement to look but there is also more opportunity to look and to strut your stuff, while all still being relatively private.

Then there are strip clubs. I have never been offended by strip clubs, well ok maybe some are quite disgusting and things happen there that I didn't need to know that a body could do – yuck, but what I mean is I was never opposed to going to one. The odd thing about that is that I never did go to one until I got a job at one. I love to say that and let people think whatever they want for a minute. Then I tell them I was just the beer bitch. I had gone to the 'All About Sex Show' one year and as we walked around in the last aisle we got into a conversation with one guy. He said he worked at one, managed it in fact. I don't know why this piqued my interest, or if I was even looking for a second job or not but when he said they were hiring, I took down his number.

I don't think he expected me to show because when I did, they had no manager by that name, they had a DJ by that name. I got the job and worked there for about three months. My first night there I didn't want to be obvious but I was certainly intrigued, I wanted to watch not work. I tried peaking over my shoulder a couple times until I noticed I was the only one doing this. Everyone-staff included, was openly staring.

From that point on I sold my beers and watched the shows. My day job found out I was working there. Mostly because I worked there Thursdays until two or three in the morning and was up at five to go to my office job. They knew I was tired on Fridays. My boss showed up a few times. That was funny as he would buy me drinks I wouldn't drink and get lap dances all night then come into work late and with a hangover. I never did dance on the stage; never even put my foot on it. I went to a couple strip clubs after that, I compared them all to the one I worked for. They often came up short, skuzzy, small, dirty and with an uneventful show. I was oddly proud of the club I had worked at.

When I went to Cali I was disappointed, in Ontario they strip completely naked, in Cali it was pasties and g strings. Vancouver hasn't impressed me yet either but I have only been to one.

Enough on that one, I once had a boyfriend tell me there was a club we could go to and have sex in public. Sounded to me like something he would do, but I didn't know if it was going to be legal. We never did it, but it remains in the back of my mind as an option.

I never thought I would say that, having being scarred many years earlier by being on the performance end unaware I was watched. But knowledge is power, and I think it would be a rush if I knew. I was around eighteen when I had a year long booty call affair with that guy. I first met him at a party and I knew I was going to sleep with him the moment I saw him. I also knew it wasn't going to be in the immediate future but it would happen. After hooking up at a party one night, we continued to hook up after hours at my place regularly, I hosted the three a.m. after party most weekends for a small crew of friends– yes Mom, I was as bad as my sister; I just hid it better.

One night after socializing had finished I pulled him up to my room. Unbeknownst to me my girlfriend was hooking up with another guy that was there and only one guy was left by himself. Rodney. I hated that name for a long time. As I was getting it on, all drunk and brazen, Rodney had come upstairs. I had crawled on top of booty call boy and was getting what I wanted with little of his help other then his permission and some approval noises. When finished, I had just flung myself over his chest and I heard a clap. My head sprung up as I rolled over for some covers and there was Rodney clapping, 'well done' he said.

To say I was humiliated, even if he was commending me, was to be putting it mildly. I had no idea if I should be embarrassed or not. I was mortified. I felt violated. The guy I was with just shook his head and went to sleep, the dick. I didn't talk to Rodney for a full year. But it's a funny story to tell now.

I still have photos of that guy somewhere. I snapped a couple when he was getting dressed once to go home. I thought of them as protection somehow. I think he was the only 'pretty boy' I ever slept with. He was gorgeous but I don't remember ever having a real conversation with him. Hmm wonder how he turned out as an adult?

19

Being Naked

<u>We were born this way</u>

I got passed my fear of nakedness when I started doing yoga. With women stripping left right and center around me I was reintroduced to the concept that not every women cares if they look like Pamela or Gisele. With that in mind, I accepted that I have a baby Buddha belly that my smaller breast will likely not sag and I have a great ass. From here I did what I was taught, embrace your fear and move past it.

I can tell you right now that there are way more photos and video of me naked out there than I am completely comfortable with. Mostly because I don't have a copy. I think it's an unfair advantage.

I was at a women's leadership class, first off let me tell you when you put a hundred women together for over a week, holy crap, it's powerful! It's amazing, liberating and enlightening and it was a perfect place to explore my insecurities and move past them – not in a sexual way, this chapter is not like that its about awareness. I stayed in a cabin with probably eighteen women ranging from young to old, all sizes and backgrounds. They were beautiful, open, funny, dynamic and supportive women. I knew I was comfortable with myself when one of the women said to me, "yes we know you want to be naked" I had spent the week wearing less and less. By the time we were painting a fence I was in a scrap of material tied over my breasts and short shorts.

When I came back from that I was feeling fantastic and when I was asked if I wanted to be in a naked photo shoot I was All over the idea. Where I would have been too shy to participate previously, I was now so excited to be a part of this incredible artistic gift that was being given to two exceptional people. A better gift could not have been thought up for them.

I was not able to be there when the gift was presented but I saw the photos of the party and the couple had been blown away by the gift. I had been emailed a link to the photos to see how they turned out. I have a group of very flexible, strong, attractive and creative friends.

This was probably the start of my being able to be naked without looking around to see who was looking. From there I remember a group vacation where Day One started off with a naked pool party that is well documented in photos. Of which my girlfriend had a few in an album on her coffee table for anyone to see.

More private photos, well they exist as well. When I was sixteen my boyfriend took shots of me in my bra and panty set. They were white with little flowers. When we broke up I asked him to destroy them. At the time I was embarrassed wondering how they turned out, I don't think of myself as very photogenic. I never saw them and I didn't want him to have pictures of me being that vulnerable. Now, I think I would be more embarrassed by the panty set. He told me he ripped them up.

Next there was a video of me and my ex boyfriend having sex. He still has it, I still want it. He is the only one I am ok with having documented pornography of me. There is something really hot about hearing yourself moaning. He had taken a bunch of photos when we were having sex and had a video option on his camera, its only fifteen to thirty seconds I think. We went to a wedding shortly there after where he lost that camera. I remember the feeling of my stomach dropping when he told me he lost the camera. I was like holy shit, are the photos on it. He was like I KNOW, good thing I uploaded before we came. Close call.

From there I had an artist friend take a set of naked photos because I was not able to sit and pose for a nude painting I had commission. It took a couple years with her moving around the country, but she sent me both the photos and then a short time later two paintings. It's not a matter of trust with her having had them. I don't think I ever care if others see them. I just I wanted to look at them too. I have become a narcissist.

When I hooked up with a previous lover after a nasty split it was easy to be comfortable with him, we already knew each others nooks and crannies but when I sent him a little reminder of what was waiting for him at home while he was away on business I surprised even myself. My spontaneous decision to show him the benefits of my waterproof bob-well, I am left feeling exposed now that we are no longer horizontal friends. At one point he asked me if I wanted him to delete them. At the time I said it was ok, and then later asked him to. I was deleting them from my computer and didn't want him to have them either.

Only, I couldn't delete them all, I wanted to keep them, so I wonder if maybe he did too. Not that I could ever erase the image from his memory, but erasing hard copy proof of my masturbation would be nice.

Ok so I am no Tracy Lords and the world has not seen all my pink parts, as much as I may strut around in front of friends I am comfortable with I am not an exhibitionist at heart. I still would not go back to the nudist resort and show off family resemblances. As for being a voyeur, well it's kind of like a car crash, can't help but look when it's in front of you and I will likely be the dirty old granny hording my erotic novels in the nursing home.

20

The Lies We Tell Ourselves

To get what we want

Where do I start? When we are born we have no idea what a lie is. Children are the most refreshingly honest souls. They don't care that it may hurt our feelings, or be embarrassing they just say what's on their minds. When did we as children get taken over to the dark side of secrets, should do's but don'ts, guilt and lies that is the bliss of adulthood?

The first lie I remember is when I was about four. I ran into my grandparents' room and crawled into their bed. I had been playing with my new necklace and the electrical socket. I don't remember how – and no I wasn't drunk, just traumatized into forgetting- but somehow I had burnt my leg, the necklace and socket had torch marks. I am guessing with brief clarity that I tried to plug it in – for what logic I cannot even imagine. When they asked me what was wrong (it was not normal for me to crawl into their bed in the middle of the night), I answered "nothing" I was in pain and I was scared of getting in trouble for ruining my brand new choo-choo train necklace. They found out in the morning when they saw my leg and the burnt chain.

My next lie I think I was around six. I told my mom I was at my friend Meredith's house, she lived across the street. I was allowed to cross if she was on the other side waiting and we both looked both ways. I had really gone down the street to another friends' and my mom couldn't find me and I wasn't in shouting distance to know that I had been caught. I confirmed my lie when asked where I was, and got in trouble.

The older I got, the more creative the lies. "No Mom nothing is wrong, I am just tired"- while I was high on pot. I think they knew and were torturing me. Parents are not as dumb as we would have them be. They were just young once too and pick and choose the punishments. Having to talk to them high was a good punishment. I was a pretty good kid. Yes I hid things from my parents but I have never been arrested, or had the police come to the house for something I did like my sister did (love you xo). The benefits of being younger is you learn from their mistakes.

As an adult though I don't need to lie to my parents, now I lie to myself. I have evolved. I have found others who do the same. If you haven't already found yourself nodding in understanding try this on. Oh I really shouldn't, when you know damn well you are going to. Who am I trying to look good for when I say that? How about, 'I'm going to be healthier this year'…yeah, right after this pint of ice cream.

I haven't gained weight my pants shrunk. We lie to ourselves all the time.

I love the pitiful justification process I went through when I was attempting to get past having once again slept with my ex when we both knew we were like crack to an addict and should have just said no. In the process of our addiction we left a trail of lies and hurt.

The lies we tell ourselves when we are not ready to have sex and do it anyway, the alcohol and drugs I have hid behind so I wouldn't have to lie, I could have an excuse instead.

The 'no' that means 'try again', the 'yes' that means 'no'. In the words of a friend, who knows me well enough to be able to say this; the 'no' that means 'fuck me baby' and the 'we shouldn't' that means 'who is going to make the move'. All of these lies just to confuse and leave room for misunderstandings. It's crazy, yet when we step outside the lies we tell ourselves that keep us in the bubble of ignorance and ask questions for clarity we get holy crap she wants commitment.

Where is it that we learned to lie to ourselves? Is it working?

21

Drama

Into everyone's life, a little drama adds flavor

This chapter is a little different. I had been in a writing slump, I lacked the desire to move forward with the book. A lot had gone on for me in the past year and I had simplified everything, I had removed all the drama, I was existing in a beautiful state of blissful peace and harmony. But since life is about balance, it found a way in; drama was inviting itself into my life by way of my friends. Though I was not dating, others were and with it they had relationship issues. I first tried to help by buying books and searching out valuable advice

Pulled from my attempt at sleeping one night, I could not shake the thoughts swirling in my head. I have gone months without drama and it had been amazing and then BAM without even recognizing it until it was all over me, there I was, engrossed in full blown, I have to write about it because people will identify - Drama! Far from being upset about it, it was worthy of a chapter and I was writing about it.

Drama is not to be feared, it's Life! In this case, it's been a catalyst.

I won't start at the beginning of this story because truthfully the beginning began on a different level and oddly enough tangled in with another chapter. We will leave it at, this tangent begins with a history in place and yet still surprisingly innocent and unknowing.

This is about me and Joe. We have been acquaintances for a number of years but only recently did we begin to notice each other, get to know each other. Think about more then friendship and spend time alone together. We had never dated and were not dating now; we just had had some laughs hanging out with each other and some significant moments where I discovered we understood each other well. If I were to write a list of all the things I am looking for in a man, Joe fits this list well. From his physical build, his personality, his past, his demeanor, his social skills, everything! At times, I felt like he was perfect for me in so many ways.

I turned around after hearing his voice, and there he was in front of me. It had been months since I last saw him, he looked good! He looked familiar, not in the obvious I know him way, but in the, my soul has known you forever kind of way. And I don't mean that in a mushy way, just in a fact kind of way, it was comfortable, it was like home.

I spent the evening over many glasses of wine catching up with friends that included him. As the evening progressed it was as if I had seen him just yesterday, like no time had passed, like I knew everything from the past months when in reality I was itching to get him alone and talk for hours and hours and hear all the longer versions of the snippets we had exchanged in emails and phone calls.

This was not the night for this though and soon the time came for me to go. As I stood behind him, my arms around him as he spoke to a friend, all I wanted was to stay there, in that moment, wrapped around him, that place that felt like home. Instead I left.

It was days later that I would see him again, and though the evening was again enjoyed with friends there was this thought in the back of my mind present with me all evening. This thought that had in truth been with me for longer then I can actually remember when it began. A thought that was I believe in alignment with his thoughts; are we going to sleep together?

It was late before those who were leaving left and then he said, "Come on, lets go to bed". Now one may think, 'Yep, they are going to sleep together', but as I said, this is not the beginning of this story and I should let you know that this is not the first time we have shared a bed, so this casual statement didn't have to mean anything other than simply what was said.

I went into the room and took off my clothes and got into bed, there was a second when I thought, what does my being naked imply. Many men would answer that question by saying 'She's offering' in this case though, I was still unsure if I was. We had slept together before, and he knew that I preferred to sleep naked. Nothing happened that time, perhaps this was going to be like that. I didn't mean to imply anything. That is the truth as I knew it in that second. I was aware in any other case it would imply something and I fully admit that I was most definitely considering what it could be implying but I wasn't sure if I wanted it to or not. I was putting it in fates hands, removing the responsibility of the situation off of me (another convenient lie I justified to myself).

He got into bed, he too was naked. We laid there a few moments talking about things I cannot even remember to quote, and even what I am about to say is paraphrasing as we all know that the he said she said versions are always subject to interpretation but it was something like; "I feel like I should pretend that this is awkward, but its not."

Though at times for this to all make sense I will need to reference the past, I promise to not go back to the true beginning and tell the entire story. But I took his words to mean, the fact that we were naked was not at all uncomfortable, quite the opposite, it was comfortable, like we did this all the time, it was natural, it was as it should be.

We'd had discussions in the past about feeling a connection that we were both perhaps surprised by. Have you even met anyone and felt an instant connection that goes so far beyond where people who have just sat to talk for the first time would generally feel? Well from day one, that is what it was like. I could not wait to see him when I knew it was a possibility. It wasn't sexual, it was just intense. It was a need to be in his presence, in his arms, within reach of him.

I remember once seeing him unexpectedly and launching myself into his arms, wrapping my legs around his waist and him twirling us around in joy. It was an unexplained and uninhibited connection.

As a result, being clothed in bed (an unnatural state for me) was...well, silly. That said, this time it was different, because this time I had been thinking about if I was going to sleep with him. Consequently, although it was not awkward, I was also not just rolling over and going to sleep. I was curious.

I cannot tell you the dialogue, because truthfully it escapes me now, nor can I share with you any other thoughts I had between the moments of getting into the bed up to the point when he had made his decision. I will tell you, the next couple minutes still bring a tremendous smile to my face and a memory that will last a lifetime for me. I will do my best to help you visualize it and convey it to you with the spontaneity it was delivered to me.

It was after midnight and both of us had to work the next day but imagine if you will, a bed, both of us lying on our backs, chatting casually, laughing on occasion. Then, with a little rustle of the sheets and some words muttered, that I can only assume now were words meant to announce his intent, I was no longer the only one on my side of the bed, in fact I was no longer the one in my exact spot on the bed. The only thing I could process was, "Uh, hello there" or some other inane statement meaning to declare that although I was indeed surprised and startled by the change of his geography, I was not opposed to it.

From here I was enveloped in the most extreme and concentrated embrace. If this was not my story, if I was an outsider unaware of the giddy feelings I had myself experienced in his presence, this could very much look like an awkward coupling of two fourteen year olds.

Instead, for me it was sweet, it was crazy and all I could do is laugh. Certainly not at him, I'm not even sure I did it out loud, but with him because I understood it to be a physical expression of what was going on for me. This transition from my excitement that this person I have such a great connection with was here with me, we were naked, we were single and there were other possibilities here if we want to....

But damn it, this was where the innocence departs and the drama enters. We were not alone in that bed. Don't get excited, I meant that mentally. There was shit going on outside the walls of that room that those same possibilities were effected by. Outside these walls there was judgment, other people's feelings and consequences. I didn't want to be considering all these things at that moment but there they were distracting me from the parade of kisses all over me. All I want to do is ignore these thoughts and enjoy what I had been considering for months. All I want to do was open my legs and let nature take its course; all I want to do was screw the world outside these walls and get some satisfaction that I had not seen in months. All I want to do is, well, slow it down and maybe catch up to where he was at and then decide what happens.

We rolled over, not gracefully, but with humor. In this moment where I was kissing his chest, stroking his body I wished that I could find the elixir that would take me back to the 'ignorant and permission filled; I just don't give a fuck attitude' I'd had in my drunken youth, when my decisions were blurred by vodka, innocence and a desire for love I thought could be found in a three a.m. screw. But this was not then, this was not a three a.m. "screw", I did care, and I couldn't do it.

If I wasn't me and he wasn't him and others we cared about wouldn't care, it could have looked like this......

Months later I was sitting in bed naked and alone, the drama had calmed down. Joe and I had continued to keep things platonic which was easy since we saw each other infrequently and communicated mostly on the phone and emails. I decided to take matters into my own hands and surprise him.

I went over to his house; I know where he keeps his hidden key. I knew he was out. I had brought a bottle of wine, opened it, made myself comfortable and watched TV for awhile until I was tired. At eleven I let myself into his room and crawled into bed and although I intended to wait up for him, I fell immediately into a deep sleep.

Reaching out with my hand in search of my phone to check the time, I wondered why I was awake when it felt like the middle of the night. My hand hit a wooden headboard. I was momentarily confused, my bed had a soft headboard, I rolled over and then remember I was not in my bed, I was in his. A little smile pulled at the corners of my mouth when I realize why I was awake. I must have heard the door, he was finally home. I had brought my shoes in the room so he didn't know yet I was there. I was chuckling to myself knowing I was about make a fantasy come true.

Maybe men don't think this way, but I know a lot of women who in those moments when they are home alone fantasize of 'prince charming' coming into their room in the middle of the night to profess their feelings and make passionate love, forgiving the reality facts of how the hell he got in your secure building, and the double lock on your apartment door.

Ok so that was not what I was going for exactly, but I would think that coming home and unexpectedly finding an attractive, naked woman in ones bed has to rank up there as pretty fucking cool, if I do say so myself.

I heard him coming down the hall, and was thinking should I play coy, feign sleeping, announce my presence, let him notice? Right about then I could've used the movie script rather than the analysis that was going on in my head. Too late, the door opened, the light shone in and he saw me there looking at him. He laughed as he entered the room, closing the door behind him. With the window shade not fully darkening the room I could see he was shaking his head in amusement.

"This is becoming habit with you" he said.

Though I hadn't seen him lately for any habits to be recent, when it came to me in his bed, this was true, it was not the first time I had come over uninvited and made myself at home. I would feel bad for invading his space without warning again if I hadn't been there naked in his bed knowing he was about to get lucky.

"Well, if at first you don't succeed…." I replied instead. The last time I came here he was the one in bed and it was me coming in. That time too there was little sleep to be had, but getting lucky hadn't been in the cards on that night either. That was an area that I was not planning on becoming habit.

Laughing, he responded, "What are you looking to succeed at? Valid question to ask, poor man, as I said I had slept here too many times with no 'happy ending'.

"I have told you once before that I had been reprimanded for not finishing what I started" I told him as I watched him undress for bed. I saw him hesitate at his pants, I wondered does he sleep naked when I was not there or was it a go with the flow thing, because even though I could tell he was not clear what was going on in my head, I knew he knew I was naked.

"Yes, I remember that message, that week had a lot of bad timing moments" he said and having apparently made his decision he took off his pants, and turned to lay them over something.

"I think fate was helping us out that week, stopping us from bad choices at the time' I said admiring his cute ass

Turning back to the bed, 'Alright, I'll buy into that, and now?'

"Well now, I think you need to be closer and I will show you how complete I can be when I finish something I start.' When he lifted the cover to slide into the bed, I elaborated, "Hope you are not tired, because I intend to go over all the fine points and make sure you are satisfied with the results"

'I like a woman who makes sure all the finer points are looked after' he quipped and moved right in and on top of me exactly where I wanted him.

I'd say again, I speak for a large portion of women when I say that there are few feelings like the feeling of the first touch of skin sliding up to skin. It's hot! In that moment he could have easily slid right into me I was so ready. Instead I wrapped my arms around his back, my legs around his hips and took his tongue into my mouth as I ground my hips against him. Why take it slow when I knew what I wanted.

As has always been the case, there was no awkward moment. It was like the past months of not being near one another (in hindsight I see that was self preservation until I could act upon my wants) evaporated. It was like I was with him just yesterday. We picked up where we'd left off.

I allowed him the dominance for awhile, it was his space I had invaded after all. I soon wanted the control and rolled on top of him. Feeling his erection firmly between us, I slid against him, enjoyed the feeling of him as excited as I was. No more hesitation, it was obvious to both of us. Somehow that left less need to hurry through. I no longer was concerned with what anyone thought.

I enjoyed his mouth. I liked kissing him. I took pleasure in playing with his tongue, lightly nipping at his lips. I could have made out with him for a good deal longer but the feel of him pressed against me was requiring more attention.

I slid down his torso, pausing only as I took his earlobe in my teeth and breathed warm air in, causing him to shiver. I kissed his neck on my way to suckle his flat nipples into my mouth for a moment. My hands going before me, I grasped his hard cock in my hand before I guided him into my hungry mouth. I took him into the warm wet heaven without preamble, shocking him, pushed his limits. Engulfing him to the back of my throat and began to stroke him with my whole mouth as I slid him out and sucked him back in. I held onto him firmly at the base, cupping his balls into my hands and slid my grasp up as I took him out from my mouth. My hand was wet from the repeated action providing a slippery track as I stroked him continually.

I stroked with my right hand and I bent and took his balls into my mouth, my other hand caressing his thigh, his ass, anywhere I could stimulate him further. I wanted to push him over the edge. I wanted to rock his world. I wanted to give this.

When his hips began to move, when his hands came to grasp at me, I took him back into my mouth, I wanted him to cum in my mouth. I alternated the pressure of my fingers on him as I stroked him in tandem with my mouth rising and swallowing him. When he put his hand to my head and said he was going to cum, I let go with my hands and continued with my mouth until I felt the first shot. I stopped my frenzied mouth action and just kept him in my mouth savoring until he was spent drinking him in.

When his hand left my head, I rose up kissed his thigh, his stomach and his neck while he regained some energy. I am good. I curled into him, rested my head on his shoulder. His hand came up to absently rub my arm. Eventually he turned his head and placed a kiss on my forehead.

"Anything else you were looking to finish? He asked

I laughed, "I have a couple other fine points on my list, if you are up to the task of helping me complete them?"

"I'm at your service", he then turned to me again and took my mouth in another passionate kiss leaving me fully aware that I too would be looked after.

I allowed that recovery for a male no longer in his twenties was going to take a little time, I was surprised how little. I was soon pushed onto my back and following some significant foreplay that left me having orgasmed not once, but twice before he thrust into me. He raised my legs higher around him and without relenting drove into me until I screamed out with number three, when I came back to this planet he turned me over and pulled me onto my knees, grabbing my hips he continued with the same momentum plunging in and out until we were both mad.

Knowing then this was not going to end soon, I backed him onto his heals and remained with my back to his front and straddled his legs. His one arm went between my legs and played with my clit, the other seized my breast, almost clutching at it. It was probably the only thing keeping me balanced as I rode him, my head back in pleasure and perspiration dripping between us. It was madness, it was intense.

I felt my legs begin to tremble and didn't think I was going to make it, only to realize it was not my legs but my insides spasming creating a vibration so powerful I could feel it in my legs. With me clenching at him, he too went over with me.

In a boneless heap we fell to the mattress and laid their regaining function.

His first words, "wanna take a shower?"